My Daniel

Also by Pam Conrad

I Don't Live Here!
Prairie Songs
Holding Me Here
What I Did for Roman
Seven Silly Circles
Taking the Ferry Home
Staying Nine

My Daniel

PAM CONRAD

HarperCollins*Publishers*

My Daniel
Copyright © 1989 by Pam Conrad

Typography by Joyce Hopkins
3 4 5 6 7 8 9 10

Libray of Congress Cataloging-in-Publication Data
Conrad, Pam.
    My Daniel / Pam Conrad.
        p.   cm.
    Summary: Ellie and Stevie learn about a family legacy when their grandmother tells them stories of her brother's historical quest for dinosaur bones on their Nebraska farm.
    ISBN 0-06-021313-2 : $ ISBN 0-06-021314-0 (lib. bdg.) : $
    [1. Brothers and sisters—Fiction.   2. Nebraska—Fiction.
3. Dinosaurs—Fiction.   4. Frontier and pioneer life—Fiction.]
I. Title.
PZ7.C76476My 1989   88-19850
[Fic]—dc19   CIP
                                                              AC

For R. C.
paleontologist and lost brother

Some of this story is true. Some of it's lies. No brontosaurus has ever been found in Nebraska, but I'm partial to Nebraska, and all my own fossils and bones come from there. And while I never heard of a young girl in Nebraska taking part in a dinosaur adventure, there was once a young girl in England in 1810 who made an important dinosaur discovery with the help of her brother.

So this story *could* have happened like it says, almost, but it didn't really, not exactly anyway.

llie's old grandmother, Julia Creath Summer-
waite, came east that summer for the first time
in her life, her own life of eighty years, and Ellie's
life of twelve. She arrived at the airport from Nebraska with
a cracked cardboard suitcase and wearing a navy-blue hat with
hard red berries on it. When she stepped off the plane and
walked down the ramp into the waiting room, her pocketbook
contained the letter Ellie's father, her youngest son, had sent
her.

All right, Momma, the letter promised. *I'll take you and
the children to the Natural History Museum and leave the
three of you there alone. Whatever you say. Just as long as
you come.*

It was the only reason she could see for coming at all.

Ellie's father had laughed at his mother's request. "I'll bet it's those old dinosaur bones," he had told his wife. "The ones from that Nebraska farm."

Ellie's mother had said how typical it was of Grandma Summerwaite to sound so mysterious, like there was some great secret in the museum, a secret she could tell only to the children.

Their parents had laughed, but Ellie and her younger brother Stevie wondered silently into each other's eyes what it was all about. They walked alongside the old woman through the walkways of the busy airport, looking up at her now and then, remembering her more from photographs than from that long-ago trip to Nebraska. She was round and soft, like an overstuffed bed, and she smelled faintly like mothballs, false teeth, and lilacs.

"So how was your trip, Momma?" Charlie Summerwaite asked. She didn't answer, and he spoke louder. "It was a clear day, huh, Momma? You had a smooth flight?"

"Yes, yes," she said grumpily. "Not as smooth as railroad tracks though. Nothing as smooth as steel rails."

"Now, Momma, you know you're too old for that long trip by train. It would've taken you days. This way you're here in a matter of hours."

"I'm too old to fly, if you ask me," she muttered under her breath. "If the good Lord had wanted me to fly He would've given me a propeller."

Ellie laughed.

"*I* took the train to Nebraska, Grandma," Stevie said, slipping his hand through the handle of her pocketbook. "But I was too little. I don't remember."

"You don't remember Nebraska?" She was shocked. "Don't you remember sitting on your daddy's shoulders when he walked you through the cornfield? Don't you remember the kittens?"

"*I* remember the kittens, Grandma," Ellie said, instantly remembering the smell of the barn and the cozy darkness. "And your quilts. I remember the quilt on my bed with the tiny little triangles all over it."

"And did you do some piecing like I showed you when you got home?" her grandmother asked.

Ellie glanced quickly at her mother and then away. She remembered how the tiny pieces of fabric had not lain flat. They had buckled and twisted and her mother hadn't known how to help her. They were still in a shoe box under her bed. "Nah, I was too little. Maybe we can start again this time. I kept the patches. You can show me again."

The long walkway finally opened into a large room with conveyor belts and signs that marked which flights would be unloading at which place. Charlie Summerwaite stood still for a minute, gazing up at them, his hands thrust deep into the pockets of his baggy tan pants. "Let's see, let's see," he mused. "Right over here. Your baggage should come out right here as soon as they unload the plane."

Stevie plopped himself down on the edge of the conveyor belt, and his parents were about to scold him and tell him to stand up when the old woman sat down next to him. "Oh, my poor feet," she sighed. Her son and his wife were silent for a moment and then, "Momma, be careful there. That belt's going to move soon."

She didn't hear him or she ignored him, and the two parents withdrew slightly. The five of them, like a small herd of buffalo, clustered into two groups according to their needs, the young children close to their grandmother.

"Did you know that clouds are born out of the rivers?" she asked them.

The children looked at her blankly.

"Did you ever wonder where clouds were born? I never did. Never thought about it, thought they just appeared out of nowhere, but I could see from the airplane, white wispy clouds rising up out of the rivers and heading over the land, just like steam coming off a jelly pot."

"Were they hot, the rivers?" Stevie asked.

"Never knew a hot river," she answered, slipping her shoes off. Ellie looked down at her grandmother's knobby feet, twisted like old tree roots, and the same color.

"And you know what else? You remember that crazy quilt I had on my bed, Elizabeth? The one with all the velvets and golden threads and no rhyme or reason, just patches all crazy?"

Ellie's face lit up. "Yes! I remember! The crazy quilt, with the black and maroon velvet patches." She could almost feel them smooth and old along the tips of her fingers.

"Well, from the sky, the Nebraska farms look exactly like crazy quilts. I swear. Now how did all those women know that? Without ever being in the sky? How did they know to make their crazy quilts look just like their husbands' farms? That's what I want to know." The old woman looked like she wanted an answer.

Ellie shrugged.

"Maybe the farmers liked the quilts *first*, Grandma," Stevie said. "And then they made their farms look like them."

She shook her head in disagreement or impatience and grew quiet. People were beginning to gather around the conveyor belt, waiting. Families, people alone, people talking excitedly, people standing without speaking to each other. None of the Summerwaites spoke now, poised at the beginning of a hopeful visit. Stevie fiddled with some stones that were in his pocket. He took them out, examined them, turned them over, and licked one.

"What have you got there, Steven?" his grandmother asked.

"His old fossils." Ellie answered for him. "He's got a whole collection. Fossils and dead bugs."

"Yeah, I wanna get a dead-bug fossil," he said, handing his grandmother one of the stones. She didn't look at it, but rather at the boy. His hair wasn't very different from the corn silk he couldn't remember. It stood out in unruly patches, and freckles marked his face like cinnamon on vanilla pudding. She could see him so clearly. Funny, but when his father had been this age she couldn't see his face like this. She had needed her reading glasses to see him up close. It was almost as if at middle age her body had resisted close things and had forced her to look outward, and now at eighty she began seeing again. She didn't even need her glasses to read anymore, as if her body were pulling her in close for one last detailed look around.

She touched Stevie's shell-shaped ear absentmindedly. "Your great-uncle collected fossils," she said. "He had a sack full of them under his bed."

"I have trays," he said. "Glass trays, and jars." And then, "What's a great-uncle?"

"A grandparent's brother. My brother, Daniel."

"Great-Uncle Daniel? Would I call him that? And he'd call me Great Steven? Does he live in Nebraska?"

"You could just call him Daniel. And he's buried in Nebraska. Not far from the river."

"Buried? He died? Was he old, Grandma, real old? Like you?"

"No. He was very young—"

Just then there was a rumbling in the conveyor belt and Charlie Summerwaite helped his mother to her stockinged feet. "Come down from there," he scolded Stevie, as the boy began to drift away atop the moving belt. "Come down right now and help your grandmother find her suitcase."

"It's got all my travel stickers on it," she told them proudly, and they waited until at last she waved at a small cardboard valise that was drifting toward them with two stickers: OMAHA and LINCOLN. Their father hoisted it off the belt and led the way out to the parking lot.

Ellie felt all light and expectant inside. Her grandmother had been with them only a short time and already she had talked about where clouds were born; about what came first, farm designs or quilt designs; and about death, about a brother who died.

Ellie sensed there would be more as they all filed through the door, one after another. It was then that she noticed her grandmother had left her shoes off and was walking along the cement barefoot like a country girl traipsing through the fields.

"Grandma! Your shoes!"

Julia Creath Summerwaite held up her shoes in one hand and with her other hand motioned Ellie to shush. "Just giving my feet a rest," she whispered. "I don't think I can get them back on right now."

Ellie smiled and took the shoes from her grandmother, slipping her hand into the old woman's. "We're having a barbecue this afternoon, Grandma. Uncle John and Aunt Betty are coming. And Lavina wants to see you. And Lillian."

"What about the museum?" she asked. "When do we go to the city?"

"Tuesday. It's all planned. We're even taking off from school for the day," Ellie told her.

"Tuesday," she echoed, squinting into the traffic of cars and taxicabs spinning through the airport. "I think I can make it till Tuesday."

O ld Julia Summerwaite and the two children made it to Tuesday. All through the weekend Ellie had plied her with questions, but no answers had come. The old woman had been quiet and almost secretive, light flashing in her eyes only at odd moments, like when Stevie showed her his rock collection, and when Ellie pulled out the shoe box filled with colorful squares. Her old fingers were too stiff to dial the phone to call Lavina or Uncle John, but the sewing needle had slipped into her hand like a sixth finger and she had whipped together a cluster of patches forming a star. Ellie had persevered, sitting by her grandmother's feet most of the time, sewing and chewing on her lip until the needle had cut a million sore little pricks in the tip of her finger, and her mother had made her put it away until she could buy Ellie a thimble.

The first sound Ellie heard Tuesday morning was the sound of rain running off the roof outside her window. At first she was afraid they wouldn't go if it was raining, but when she ran down to the kitchen, her grandmother was already there in a dark-blue dress with white polka dots and her navy-blue hat with the berries, counting her money.

"We're still going?" Ellie burst out.

"Of course. Why not?"

"It's raining. I thought maybe you wouldn't want to go out . . ."

"Nonsense. What's a little rain? Why, I remember once when I was young I had to ride around in the rain on our horse for hours trying to find an ornery cow we had. She hated rain, the little she saw of it, and as soon as it started to really pour this crazy thing would head for the hills. Only problem was, we never knew which hills."

"Do you know how to milk a cow, Grandma?"

"I know how to milk it, feed it, slaughter it, skin it, drain it, quarter it, roast it, and eat it," she answered, getting up from her seat.

Ellie's mouth twitched involuntarily. It was strange the things Gram *did* know how to do, and yet she didn't know how to drive on parkways or work TV knobs.

"Sit down, now, Elizabeth," her grandmother said, "and I'll bring you some oatmeal." She brought the steaming pot to the table, and Ellie, accustomed to instant oatmeal, watched as thick luscious oatmeal full of raisins and brown sugar was scooped into her bowl. She watched the back of the old woman as she returned to the stove and thought how her grandmother must have always been old. Always had old feet in thick black shoes, always had gnarled hands and gray hair the color of an old pewter pitcher. But just then, silhouetted in the early light of the kitchen window, Julia Creath Summerwaite touched the back of her neck with a soft finger and tucked a strand of hair up beneath her bun. And for an instant Ellie was hardly aware of, she saw what her grandmother must have been like when she was a young girl. A young farm girl in Nebraska.

Charlie Summerwaite pulled the family station wagon before the impressive building of the Natural History Museum. Ellie and Stevie gazed out from the back windows. On the wide stairway to the entrance was a statue of a man on horseback on a huge pedestal. The rain had stopped, but he was slick and shiny against the gray sky. While people hurriedly trotted up the steps or walked lazily down them, this bronze man stood stock-still, his naked African companion walking at his side, frozen, and the horse caught midstride. Ellie stared at them, and the rider stared over her head and past her, past the park, beyond the river, all the way out to some African plains that only he could see.

"I'll be back here at five, Momma, all right? Right here in front, exactly where I'm dropping you off now. There'll be a lot of traffic, so you just wait and I'll be along."

His mother peered out at the entrance and the statue. "This is the only entrance? There isn't another one just like it on the other side? I know Mabel left me at Brandeis Department Store once to do some shopping, and don't you know, there were about six doors in, and I just thought we'd never find each other."

"Don't worry, Momma. This is the main entrance. You'll see the statue there. Wait at the statue." He turned and looked back at the children. "You two be good for Grandma now, you hear? I don't want to get any bad reports. Stevie! Are you listening?"

"Yes, Dad."

"And if you want to come home early, just call, and I'll come right in and get you. All right? You have enough money now, Momma?"

She ignored him and fumbled for the car-door handle. "Five o'clock, Charles, at the statue. Go on about your business. We won't be needing you."

The children followed her out of the car and up the marble steps that led to the entranceway. She had to stop twice along the way to take deep breaths and adjust her pocketbook. Ellie stayed at her side, but Stevie took the steps in bounds until he was at the top beside large stone panels of a buffalo herd in profile, forms that seemed pressed into warm sandlike fossils.

"Look, Gram!" he cried. "Buffalo! Did you have any buffalo on your farm in Nebraska?"

"Oh, I'd seen one or two come wandering by in my day, when I was real young," she answered, coming up alongside him. She ran her fingers along their shapes. Did she really remember, she wondered? More than remembering the buffalo, she remembered her arms wrapped around her father's neck that day as he ran, leading her mother and her brother Daniel up over the hills. Her father had come home from the fields dirty and sweaty and had run into their soddy, calling them out. "This might be the last one," he was shouting as he scooped her up and began running. His scratchy beard rubbed against her cheek as she held tight, her teeth rattling, and over his shoulder she watched as Daniel followed, his legs pumping wildly up the hills, and the sun bouncing off his straw hair. "There used to be hundreds, thousands!" he was telling them. They came to the crest of the hill and he seemed to squeeze her even tighter to him.

"Look," he whispered.

Their mother had come up alongside them, hands clutching her apron, wisps of her curly hair whipping around her face in the wind, and Daniel, so ferocious and brave, had gathered up pebbles from the ground and had begun to chuck them in the direction of the lone buffalo. "Giddap, git, you ugly ole cow!"

"Stop that, Daniel," his father ordered, and Daniel stopped, the stones slipping from his fingers. "He doesn't even hear you. Look how old he is. How lonely."

She had a vague memory of that buffalo now, but it wasn't clear, more a memory of a matted brown sadness moving alone over her gray farm, as she watched from the timelessness of her father's arms. The memory that was most clear was the sudden trembling of her father's ribs against her, and a torn sob or hiccough that came from beneath his mustache. She had looked away from the buffalo then, and had clung with both arms to her father's neck as she looked back in the direction of the soddy.

"Come on, Gram," they were saying. She looked down now at the two children who were staring up at her, and wondered for an instant who they were. "Come on. Let's go in," they said. She nodded, remembering, and followed them to the revolving doors.

The three of them fit in the opening, and pushed with all their might to turn the door around and release themselves into the main lobby. "Goodness," she said, "you'd think they didn't want anybody coming in with doors like that. How would you two ever have gotten in if I wasn't here?"

"You did good, Gram," Stevie said, patting her soft arm muscles. "You did real good."

Suddenly aware of where they were, they grew quiet. Inside seemed somehow even bigger than outside. A high ceiling embossed with leaves and wedding-cake moldings arched way over their heads, higher than the tree in their backyard, Ellie thought, the pine tree that scratched the stars on dark winter nights. And at each end were large windows where soft light streamed in and lit the murals on the walls, murals of warriors, people, animals, and jungles. The room echoed with voices and footsteps—a cathedral where no one had been told to be quiet. Stevie threw back his head and yodeled into the air, his voice filling the vast room. Louder and louder.

"Stevie, hush," Ellie scolded, jerking his sleeve, so he turned to face her.

But his mouth formed a perfect *o* and his wailing howls continued as his echoing voice chased itself around the ceiling.

"Steven Summerwaite," his grandmother said, narrowing her eyes and bending toward him, "can you go over there where all those pamphlets are and see if you can find me a map of this place?"

Ellie and her grandmother watched as Stevie skipped across the marble floor, sending his crowings and yodels into the air. They watched as he approached the information stand, and then watched as a guard came over to Stevie, placed a hand on his shoulder, and the yodels stopped.

"Serves him right, the big baby," Ellie muttered, feeling obedient and righteous as she stood next to her grandmother.

"Now, now, Elizabeth, he's just a little boy. You know you'd probably enjoy giving a good whoop in here yourself, now wouldn't you? I know *I* would."

Stevie ran back to them with a brochure in his hand. "The guard said this one has a floor plan. Right here." His grandmother sat down on a wide stone bench and he opened it like a treasure map on her lap. Ellie wandered off a little. The thick reddish-brown stone pillars made her feel tiny. They were so huge that if they had made a noise they would have roared. She wanted to wrap her arms around one of them, but she didn't. *She* knew how to behave in a museum. Instead, she ran her fingers over the pillars. They were cold and still.

"All right, Elizabeth," the old woman called to her. "I see

where we have to go, and the last stop will be the fourth floor.
So we'll work our way up slowly and see what we see." The
old woman was smiling.

"The dinosaurs are on the fourth floor?" Ellie asked.

"Never you mind now," she answered.

"Aren't you going to tell us why you brought us here,
Grandma?"

"Of course I am," she said, standing and tucking her pocketbook under her arm. "As we go, so I can tell you the whole
story. Now where is that brother of yours?" Stevie had suddenly disappeared.

They looked around them, and there, off to the side, stood
Stevie in the center of a group of bronze natives who held
their shields high over their heads. At his feet was a lion, a
dead lion pierced with a sword. Frozen, arms high, he smiled.
"I'll bet you can't see me," he said as they approached.

"Stevie," Ellie hissed. "Get down from there before the
guards catch you and kick us out. What did Daddy tell you?
You are going to be in so much trouble. You never listen."

"Aw, you wouldn't have found me if I hadn't said anything."

"Right, you just blended right in with all those naked stat-
ues. Looks like the four of you were just waiting for a bus in
the rain." Ellie rolled her eyes and glanced around for a guard
as Stevie jumped down from the high ground the natives stood
on.

"My brother Daniel never listened much either," Stevie's
grandmother said, patting down the collar on his shirt.

"Was he always getting in trouble, Gram?" he asked.

"Oh, no," she answered, her voice growing soft. "He was pretty smart. He didn't get into too much mischief. Once I remember he almost got a whopping, though, for not paying attention to the planting." Her mind wandered back to the swells and rolls of the Nebraska prairie farm.

One morning Daniel and I were following behind Ma and Pa out in the fields. I was too little to really do much useful work, but I was big enough to follow along. I thought it was fun in those days to see Pa strapped to a plow like a horse, a workhorse that plodded along wordlessly while Ma steered the plow through the hard soil. I was too little to understand how poor we were.

I remember how everything was so slow and thick—the air, the sky, the dirt; Daniel's job was to plant the seeds. I followed along beside him through the heavy clods of dirt and watched as he dropped one seed after another before each of his bare feet. Daniel carried a sack full of seeds on his shoulder, and it seems I can remember him pulling a dry twig or flower out of the sack and tossing it at me with a big grin. The grin. I search my memories for the exact slant of his smile.

And then suddenly Daniel dropped to his knees in the soil. I crouched next to him, my hand on his knee, and watched as he pulled rocks from the dirt. The rocks were the size of the palm of my hand, and there—hundreds and hundreds of miles from any seashore—he had licked his fingers and, darkening the surfaces of the rocks, brought life to the delicate designs of clams and tiny seashells.

"Look, Julie," he had said, holding it out to me. But as I reached for it, it had flown from his hand as Pa caught Daniel by the back of the neck and jerked him to his feet.

The harness straps were wrapped around my father's chest and shoulders like thick suspenders. Above him the greenish clouds swelled in the sky, and lightning cut through them like tiny stabs of blood.

"You think I'm just some kind of workhorse, son? You think I like doing an ox's job while you play in the dirt? Where are the seeds for the last row?"

"Right here, Pa." Daniel looked worried, patting the sack against his side. "There were fossils, Pa, clear ones—"

"Fossils!" our father had shouted. Sweat dripped off his chin, and his hands trembled as he unbuckled his belt and drew it out of his pants.

"Doug, Doug," our mother said, wrapping her fingers around his wrist. "Come on," she coaxed, "come on." She drew him away from us, pulling him by his harness, leading him in the direction of the soddy. "Let's rest," she said. "Eat."

We watched our parents walk away, our mother circling Pa's waist with her arm. Then he turned back and shouted at us. "Get those seeds in that last row, you hear me?"

"Yes, Pa, yes!" Daniel was on his feet and running, dropping a seed before each foot.

I had gathered up the fossils and put them in my pockets to save for Daniel. And I remember it wasn't long after that

that Pa bought Daniel a chisel and a shovel for his fossils. I guess he was sorry.

"So he never got into any *real* trouble, Grandma?"

Julia Creath looked into the unfamiliar girl's face, surprised to see her there. Where was young Daniel's face? "What? No, he didn't get into trouble. I just said my father gave Daniel a chisel and a shovel. To dig for fossils."

"But before you said he never listened. He got in trouble."

"Oh, maybe a little now and then," she answered, rubbing her eyes and trying to clear her thoughts, to pull herself away from the smell of the soil and the green stormy light. "But nobody could stay mad at Daniel long," she said quietly. "He was that way. And after he got his chisel he was always down by the river looking for fossils."

"Like me," Stevie said. "Only I don't have a river. I have a creek though, and a school yard. Come on, Gram, I wanna find the Indians, see?" He pointed to a picture in the brochure.

Their grandmother looked carefully at the brochure. "That's on the floor below us," she told him. "Let's go down there and begin at the beginning. We'll work our way up to the dinosaurs."

"Tell us, Grandma," Ellie begged. "Start the story now about the dinosaur."

The old woman began to wander out of the lobby toward the stairs. The children followed. "Well, to begin, it happened long ago."

She leaned into the banister as she led them down the stone stairs. Ellie touched the cold brass banisters lightly and stared at the bottoms that ended in faces of dangerous tigers.

"Dinosaurs happened real, *real* long ago, Gram," Stevie told her.

"Well, I only know the part where we came in. Where the dinosaur in the dry creek bank met the two children from the farm. I was about twelve years old by then, same as you, Elizabeth, and Daniel was almost sixteen, with legs like a colt's and a shadow of a beard beginning on his cheeks. I always remember his age, 'cause it was me who got to tell the stone-cutter—Daniel Creath, December 16, 1869–October 25, 1885. And that last year was just about the worst year for Nebraska farmers. All the farms were over-mortgaged, and it hadn't rained in three years."

"Three years? Not at all?"

"Well, maybe a few fat drops that sizzled in the sand after they'd paid some Indians to do a rain dance, but nothing to speak of. Nothing to run a farm on. And the year before the drought began, my father's whole crop was eaten by locusts. Bugs that flew in one afternoon and ate everything."

"They ate everything?" Stevie whispered.

"Just about. My mother gave us each a sack to beat them off, to try to keep them away from our vegetable garden at least. But they were like smoke. All over. In my hair. Up my sleeves. On my legs. I remember running into the soddy to hide under the bed. But they were even under there. The worst part was my mother when it was over."

"Why?"

"She was wearing her favorite dress. It was green and white stripes with a high tight collar, and she was thin and pretty then. But the locusts had liked the green stripes. Guess they thought they were leaves, and they ate all the green right out of her dress before they lifted up and passed through. She came into the soddy and when I looked out from under the bed she was sobbing and gasping and all she was wearing was the white stripes that were left on her dress."

"The bugs ate her dress?" Stevie cried.

"I hate when mothers cry," Ellie whispered.

The old woman slipped her arm around Ellie's shoulders and looked at her. "It's worse when they won't cry," she said sadly.

Stevie called out from behind them, "Hey! Look at the old eyes on this dodo bird!" They turned to follow Stevie, but the old woman paused before a glass case where a flock of flamingoes and egrets was suspended mid-flight before a yellow-orange sky. Their long feet dragged in the air.

"What do you mean, when they won't cry?" Ellie asked.

The old woman squinted up at the flamingoes and egrets. "It was the day the sandhill cranes came to Nebraska," she said quietly, the birds in flight stirring her thoughts like a pebble tossed in the creek. "In the spring. I remember the swarms of cranes hovering over the horizon, slow wavering lines in the sky. I remember watching them that early morning from the front door of the soddy, while my mother gave birth to the third baby that died."

"Died? Why'd it die, Grandma?" Ellie's face glowed in the light of the flamingoes, and a group of small school children marched by, their echoing voices and footsteps coming first and leaving last.

"Who knew? Babies were born and they either lived or they didn't. It was hard on the women, though, when so many died. Guess they didn't expect much after a while."

"Was that baby a boy or a girl?"

"A boy. Like Daniel. I lost two brothers that year. He lived a little while though. Not long. Long enough for the morning shadows to grow short. But before he died, I went in to my mother, and he was all wrapped up and she held him in one hand like a kitten. He was so tiny that Momma's wedding ring fit over his fist."

The old woman and the young girl continued walking, their eyes on a little boy up ahead.

"Your mother. She didn't cry?"

The old woman squinted back in time. "No. She didn't. But a couple of days later she stood in the doorway of the soddy and said the strangest thing. Maybe it would've been better if she cried."

"What did she say?"

"She was looking east, staring at the horizon, and she said more to herself than to me, she said, 'Sometimes, Julie, I think I could walk home. Just leave my apron on the hook, step out this door here, and walk all the way home.' Funny, but I didn't know what she was talking about then. Walk home? She was standing in the doorway of our home, but I never forgot it, and it wasn't till years later that I realized she was talking about walking back to Pennsylvania where she'd been born. That's what she was thinking about. Our soddy wasn't home to her, even then. Can you imagine that? And Daniel and I'd both been born there." They walked on in silence, past a glassed-in bird sanctuary with blooming dogwood and a snow scene of deer in the woods. Stevie urged them on through the museum, past glowing displays of giant earthworms and ants, and hardened jellyfish that hung like delicate Christmas balls in lit cases.

Soon they came into a bright room, and there in the center stood a long canoe filled with hard brown Indians rowing silently, a whole tribe rowing nowhere. "I have to rest my feet, Elizabeth." Ellie and her grandmother sat on a bench on the side of the canoe room, and the old woman slipped her shoes off while the young girl's feet swung patiently below her.

Stevie circled the canoe. The brown leathery Indians didn't move. Some stood, some sat paddling or pushing with long sticks, and a couple just gazed down into the murky water that wasn't there. They held their poses faithfully. And in their silence Julie Creath began to speak. Not in a gruff way, as if her words cost money and she had none to spare, but rather her words flowed like a Nebraska summer wind, without effort, as if she were singing a song she'd been practicing all her life.

"I loved my brother, Daniel," she began. "Loved him with a white fire. And like a burnt-out buffalo chip will crumble into dust if you stomp your foot beside it—that's what I was like once Daniel was gone. I never loved anyone like that again. And I always knew that one good jolt would've robbed me of my form and I'd have been nothing more than dust in a prairie wind.

"That's how much I loved my brother, and yet, even now, these years later, I have forgotten his face, and there's no photoprint, no sketch to bring him back to me. Only my memories, and in these he is faceless—his shoulder disappearing behind the rump of the cow, his legs churning up the side of the soddy roof, or his hands, that day, limp and lifeless in the brown grass, up by the graveyard of dragons."

"A graveyard of dragons, Grandma?"

"The dinosaur," she said simply, looking down at the child. "Did you ever hear of anything so crazy as looking for a dinosaur and then finding it? But that's what my brother did. He was determined to find one, and then that freak spring rain came after three years of nothing, filling the old buffalo wallows with brown mud, making the farmers crazy with hope, and washing away whole chunks of prairie grass and soil that lined the dry creek on our farm. And there they were. Bones. Hard and heavy, and big. So big, and Daniel knew just what they were, 'cause he'd been looking for them ever since that winter night when Pa had first told us about them."

Julie Creath could feel the coarse wood of their kitchen table under her hands as she sat near the stove with Daniel and listened to her father talk about the dinosaurs and the dinosaur hunters for the first time. She could hear the ice on the river cracking like gunfire in the distance. Her mother was standing over the stove, softly chopping onions, potatoes, and dried meat. She was listening, too, and the baby was just beginning to show, the one that died in the spring.

"He was a real city slicker, that Howard Crow," Pa was telling us. "With hands like a woman and shiny shoes. A *paleontologist*, he called himself. And he told the most incredible story. But some folks will say it isn't so incredible at all." We were startled by my father's laugh, we heard it so seldom those days. "Who knows," he went on. "That Crow sure did seem to know an awful lot about fossils and bones. And according to him and some others, there may be more than scrawny corn and rattling sunflowers in this damned Nebraska soil."

"Doug," Momma scolded.

"The land *must* be damned, Maggie. Why else would it lie dry for years, turning seeds to dust."

"But, bones, Pa? What did he mean, *bones*?" Daniel tilted forward on the small barrel he was sitting on.

"He claimed that years ago—now we're talking years and years ago, thousands, maybe even millions—gigantic reptiles walked across America."

"Big as a soddy?" I asked.

"Bigger. They could step on a soddy and flatten it."

"But what's a reptile?"

"Like a lizard," Daniel answered to quiet me.

"And he said that these giant reptiles—"

"Giant lizards!" I cried, suddenly seeing it all so clearly in my imagination. "You mean dragons? There were dragons walking around right here in Nebraska?" I peered over my father's shoulder and out the deep soddy window, past my mother's geraniums.

"Would you hush," Daniel said, giving my braid a tug that jerked my head. And I hushed.

"That's what he said," my father answered. "He said they are extinct now. Dead and gone. Not a single one left, kind of like the buffalo will be soon. But sometimes they find the petrified bones of them buried in riverbanks, or in hills. Bones that have turned to stone over the years. They've found whole entire dinosaurs, head to tail in New Jersey, the Wyoming territory, and even as close as Kansas. And then they put the bones together and rebuild them."

"Imagine," Daniel said, his eyes growing soft and gentle in the kerosene light. "Maybe right here on our own farm. Giant bones."

Pa's face grew cynical and creased with his hard smile. "Now that would be something. I can imagine what they pay in the museums back east for bones like that."

"They pay? How much?" Daniel suddenly sat tall, like a prairie dog smelling the wind.

"Hundreds, I bet. Who knows? Crow left his address with everyone he met and said to watch for bones, and if ever any of us were to find any, we could write him and he'd come take a look. And there'd be a reward."

"Do you still have his address, Pa?"

"Maggie, where'd we put that paper?"

Momma frowned and said, "Now, Doug, why are you getting that boy all stirred up with pipe dreams?" But she turned from her stove and reached up on the shelf behind the coffee mill. She brought down scraps of paper, and pulled one out, handing it to Pa.

"*Howard Crow,*" he read, flattening it on the table before him. "*Please notify at once in the event of the discovery of any unusual fossils, bones, or other unidentifiable stones. Reward for exclusive rights to findings.*"

"Now, wouldn't that be something?" Pa said. "We wouldn't even have to plant this year. We could pay off the two mortgages, get us some strong stock—"

"And what good does that do, thinking like that?" Ma said, her voice brittle with anger that I didn't understand then. I didn't know yet how dreams had turned to bitter fruit for her.

"When was he here, Pa?" Daniel asked quietly, getting up to read over his father's shoulder. They both ignored my mother, who went about her cooking, banging the pots a little louder, slicing potatoes a little surer. Daniel and my father became like two men, talking business. I felt left out.

"Oh, a few years ago. I just thought of it because I heard there were some dinosaur prospectors again up in Cherry County right now poking around. Looking for bones in this area. Heard they were coming this way."

"But what if they're not all dead," I whispered. "What if there are still one or two dragons wandering around the sand hills, eating buffalo, squashing soddies . . ."

For an instant I think I see Daniel's face. Leaning on his

hand, smiling at me, his sister. "Sometimes, Julie," he says, "sometimes I think you talk just to hear your face go."

And it was later that spring that the heavy rains came. Heavy rains that exposed what Daniel and I thought was the treasure of a lifetime. But truth is, what came with it was worse than any fire-breathing dragon I could ever have dreamed up.

I can remember that spring morning Daniel got me up to go fishing with him and Jarvis Summerwaite."

"Jarvis Summerwaite! Who's that, Gram?" Stevie had left the canoe and come up next to his grandmother. He took the two shoes she had slipped out of and placed them beside her on the bench.

"Jarvis was Daniel's best friend," she told him. "He lived close enough to come by pretty often."

"But Summerwaite's *my* name," he said.

She seemed flustered for an instant. "Well, yes, that too. But that was later. He's your grandfather, but first he was Daniel's friend."

"He's dead too, Gram?"

"Stevie!" Ellie scolded. "Stop asking if everybody's dead."

"Yes, Stevie. Jarvis Summerwaite is dead, but he lived a good long life." She was smiling. "Grew a beard like Daniel never did, had children like Daniel didn't, and always remembered my brother. He'd say, 'Isn't it too bad, Julia, that Daniel isn't here?' and 'Wouldn't Daniel have gotten a kick out of that, Julie?' "

"Did you go fishing at a pier, Gram?"

"No, to the river."

That morning Daniel nudged me in the dark. He sat me up in bed, slipped an old sweater over my nightshirt, and guided my feet into a pair of his old overalls that were too small for him. And too big for me. I could've done it myself, but I used to like when he babied me. I think he liked babying me now and then, too. He liked kneeling before me and rolling up the legs of my overalls till my scrawny ankles stuck out like a crow's.

I pretended I was still sleeping while I was standing, and quietly, with just the rustling of our clothes and our bare feet scuffling along the packed-dirt floor, Daniel led me out into the cool morning darkness where we could hear the windmill rod pumping up and down in the soft wind. Someone hiding 'round the corner of our soddy made a sound like a frog. But I knew it was Jarvis. I was always smarter than Jarvis.

They made me carry the pail of worms, and the two of them

carried the fishing rods and lines. It was a long walk and the morning was chilly. Jarvis whistled into the darkness. I knew Daniel wouldn't hold my hand with Jarvis there, so I didn't try. I was never much for fishing, even then, so once we got to the river, I just lay down on the thick grass under a cottonwood and listened to the sun come up and the birds coming to life. Once the sun was pounding down on us and the morning was growing warm, I started to think. I asked Daniel if Ma knew where we were.

"She'll figure it," he answered.

"Daniel!" I shouted. "You mean you didn't tell her we'd be down here?"

"Nope. Nobody needed me for nothing today. Pa's to town. Already did my chores last night. The rest can wait for later."

"Well, I didn't do *my* chores! Ma's gonna skin me."

"Julie, Julie, Julie," he sighed, with his crazy lopsided grin that made me hate him and love him.

"Fine for you, Daniel. You won't get in trouble no matter what. You'll come marching in with your smelly fish like some hero. But what about me?"

"Pick some flowers for Ma."

"Daniel!" I stamped my foot.

But I decided to give it a try. When Jarvis waded out into the river to cast out one last time, closer to the fish that jumped near the rocks, I walked back into the trees and searched for spring wildflowers. Daniel'd hold out his catch, and Ma would praise him, and I'd hold out my bouquet and I'd get a shouting for letting the eggs sit that morning.

I looked back now and then at Daniel there on the bank, his long body stretched out in the grass, his pole tilted from the pocket of his arm, and his knee pointing to the sky like an arrow. I liked knowing where he was. It was always like that with me, ever since I could remember. But I wandered farther away than I meant to, out of sight, until I heard footsteps coming out of the trees. Jarvis stepped into the sun, his pole under his arm, and one long fish hanging from a line on his shoulder.

"Gotta get back," he said, barely looking at me, not stopping.

"Where's Daniel? He coming?" I asked.

"Prob'ly." And he walked on in the direction of his farm.

I looked after Jarvis and then into the trees. Daniel wasn't coming. I picked some more flowers. There weren't many yet. And looked back again. And I suddenly started to wonder if casting out, maybe Daniel had slipped and smacked his head on a rock, and was lying there with bubbles coming out of his nose and little minnows pecking at his hair.

He wasn't coming. A solitary hawk dipped toward the sun right over me. And just as I was about to toss the flowers aside and run back to him, Daniel stepped out of the trees, the bucket and pole in one hand and a couple of fish hanging from the other. He passed me without a word and I stepped in behind him, watching him walk. His shoulders were wide and strong, almost like Pa's, but the tendons of his ankles were still fine and delicate like the inside of a chicken's wing. And suddenly, I don't know, I wanted to cry.

I caught up with Daniel to show him my flowers, and I slipped my arm around his waist. He didn't seem to mind, now that Jarvis was gone, and I didn't mind the wet fish slapping up against my leg. 'Cause nothing bad could ever happen to me and Daniel. Ever. I wanted to think we were like the boulders down by the river—unmovable, strong, eternal. Even if something should happen to Ma and Pa, I knew nothing bad would ever happen to us. We'd always be just as we were that morning.

Funny how I remember thinking that then, because on the road back we met those dinosaur prospectors Pa had heard about, and that was the beginning of everything. Or as I think of it now, maybe the end.

"Howdy, there!" one of them called out.

We turned around to see two men coming up the road toward us. They were on horseback, and although they looked dirty and tired, even I knew they had a sort of rich look about them. They weren't farmers. One wore a big expensive hat like a cowboy, and the other had a raccoon hat. Their jackets were of fine leather, and their boots were decorated with patterns and stitching. They came up to us, smiling.

"Get a good catch this morning?" the raccoon man asked, eyeing Daniel's line. I could see their packs were loaded.

"Good enough," said Daniel. "Should be a few more in the river. Help yourself."

The cowboy looked through the trees toward the river. "Not a bad idea," he said to himself. "I sure could use a bath, too."

"This your place?" the raccoon man asked.

"Yep," Daniel answered. "Two hundred sixty acres."

"Corn and wheat?" The cowboy looked at me.

"Sunflowers and crickets, Pa says," I answered.

They laughed, easy laughs.

"I'm Daniel Creath. This here's my sister."

"Julie," I told them.

"Brett Holloway," said the cowboy, touching his hat.

"Jim Rhoades," said the raccoon man, nodding.

"Think we can camp on your land for a few nights while we look around?" Brett asked. "Maybe by the river?"

"Don't see why not," Daniel answered. "Come up and see my pa." Daniel pointed in the direction of our soddy.

"Thank you, son. We're just going to set up a tent with our equipment, get washed, and we'll be up."

"Equipment?" Daniel and I asked in unison.

"Picks, shovels, maps."

"What do you do?" Daniel asked, but didn't we both already know?

"We hunt dinosaurs." Jim smiled. "You probably don't even know what they are."

"Hell I don't," Daniel swore. He actually stepped forward and grasped the rein on Jim's horse. "Are you the prospectors been up in Cherry County this winter?"

The two men looked at each other. "How'd you hear about that?"

"My pa heard. In town."

"He hear it from Hump, do you know?"

"Hump? Don't know any Hump."

"Nobody's been through here on a camel?"

I laughed. "A camel! Not since the three wise men passed through following a star."

Brett looked at my brother and grinned. "Funny kid you got there."

"Funny as a pump," Daniel said, and then, "come up to the house as soon as you're settled. Pa's gonna be real glad you're here."

"You got it," Brett answered, touching his long finger to the brim of his hat.

"And, sir . . . " Daniel was suddenly polite and tense.

"Yes?"

"Think I could see your . . . equipment?"

"Don't see why not."

"I've got a pick and shovel," he told them.

"What for?"

"Fossils."

"No kidding." I saw the two men look at each other again.

"Find anything good?" Jim asked.

"Sure. I got some good stuff."

"Well, tell you what, young fellow, you get out your fossil collection to show us and we'll give you a tour of our tent first chance we get."

"Right!" Daniel nearly jumped out of his skin. He patted the horse on the nose and released the reins. "See you back at the soddy," and then he pretty near left me in his dust, he was in such a hurry to get back there and clean up his collection.

"Daniel," I called after him. He didn't hear me. "Daniel! Wait for me!"

But Daniel was strides ahead of me already. Worlds ahead.

I remember when Daniel had dug the grave for our little brother earlier that spring. He had to do it because Pa was gone to town for a few days to buy supplies, borrow more money, and make more empty promises. By the time Pa came home everything was over. He never got to see the baby, little as he was, and Ma had already had her queer moment of standing in the doorway dreaming about "going home."

So Daniel dug the grave on top of a hill overlooking the river, on the common ground where there were other graves, other stories. I remember the wind, the wind always blowing there, as if it were trying to wear away the names on the couple of tombstones that had been shipped in from far away and carried up the hill in carriages. Daniel's buried there today, and now there's a tall black fence around it, but when the sun is setting, the cedar trees are exactly the same as they were then—tall, scraggly, and casting black shadows over the hollows and rises.

Daniel kept digging. The ground was hard and cold, and I sat nearby, watching the dirt fly up in hard chunks as Daniel sank lower and lower into the hole. "Oh, Daniel, come up. Come up," I begged. "Daniel. That's deep enough." But he didn't answer me and he went deeper and deeper. "You don't have to go that deep, Daniel."

"There are wolves," he said. "Has to be deep."

"But you won't be able to get out."

"He's our brother, Julie. It's supposed to be deep."

"You're not digging a grave, Daniel. You're digging a well."

Finally he was still. The dirt stopped flying. His breathing quieted and I waited there in the grass. "Daniel?"

"Look at this, Julie," he said from the hole.

I crept over to it and looked down at the top of his head. He was bent over something. In his hand he held what looked like a pale stiff fish. I flattened myself on the cold ground to get a closer look, my head hanging over my brother's grave.

"Look," he said, holding it up to me. He rubbed his finger over part of it, and three white teeth gleamed up out of the hole. "A jawbone."

"Maybe a dinosaur," I suggested, remembering my father telling us about them that winter.

"Dinosaurs are bigger," he told me. "This is probably just an old cow or something."

Daniel handed it up to me with the shovel and hoisted himself out of the grave. How easily he had gotten out of *that* one.

And then, a month later, there we were sitting with those two dinosaur prospectors in our very own soddy. It was late afternoon, and Ma had lit the lamp. The table was strewn with rocks and shells and odd little stones that looked like piles of buttons. Brett was holding the jawbone from the grave in his hands.

"No, this isn't even fossilized," he was saying. "Not turned to stone yet. It's still just a bone, probably a few hundred years old, though. A bison would be my guess."

"Any of these unusual?" Pa asked, touching his hands to Daniel's collection. Daniel stood by, waiting, holding his breath.

Jim drew the biggest, heaviest-looking stone toward him. He dug a little at it with his fingernail, and dirt fell away. He pulled a small brush out of his pocket and fussed at it a bit. "This is nice. You know what it is, don't you?" he asked.

"Turtle shell?" Daniel guessed.

"Right. Probably over a million years old."

"A million years." Daniel reached out and touched it. The white million-year-old powder clung to his fifteen-year-old fingers.

"Nothing here that looks like dinosaur, though," Brett was saying. "Old. You've got some old stuff, that's for sure, but nothing big, or nothing that looks like it comes from anything big."

"Where do you look for dinosaurs?" Daniel asked. "I want to find one."

Jim and Brett laughed.

"No! I really do!" my brother cried, and I wanted them to take him seriously, not to laugh.

"Oh, we believe you, Danny-boy," Brett said. "We believe you all right. You and a few others want to find one."

"Who else?" Pa asked. "What's going on right now? You know I met Howard Crow once—"

"Crow!" Jim looked up from the turtle shell in shock. "When was Crow out here?"

"Oh, it must have been ten years ago or so."

I felt the two dinosaur prospectors relax. "He's paying us to cover the area," Brett explained. "Couldn't figure why he would have come out here himself."

"Unless he was checking up on us." Brett and Jim looked at each other.

"Why would he do that?" Daniel asked.

"Nasty business, this dinosaur hunting," Brett was saying. He stuck his brush back in his pocket and began putting the fossils back in their sacks. "There's a dinosaur war going on, if you really want to know. Crow and our old employer, Oswald Mannity, are trying to outsmart each other. For years. To see who can find the most dinosaurs, name the most dinosaurs, and rebuild the most dinosaurs." He shook his head and laughed. "Ever see two little brats fight over a toy? That's what the two of them are like. Crow has more money than he knows what to do with, and Mannity hasn't the personal fortune, but he's got the pull in all the right places."

Jim leaned his chair back against the soddy wall and grinned at us. "Not to mention he's a sneaky, low-down dirty dog who'll do just about anything short of slitting his mother's throat to get his hands on a dinosaur before Crow does."

None of us were grinning. Ma was very still.

Brett went on. "Once Crow found this giant saurian, had it reconstructed back east, and don't you know, Mannity discovers Crow's got the head on the wrong end. He put it on the end of the tail instead of the end of the neck, and, hell, Mannity never let him hear the end of it."

Pa cleared his throat.

"You say you used to work for this Mannity fellow?"

"Yep," Jim answered. "Brett and I worked for him for a couple of years. So we know firsthand the kind of filthy rotten snake he is."

"And then Crow came along and offered us twice the money," Brett added, and he and Jim laughed.

"Yes, sir," Jim said, still laughing. "And you couldn't meet a nicer guy. A real chip-eating saint." They were both laughing so hard that Daniel and I just sat there with dumb grins on our faces, looking at them. Ma began fussing furiously at the stove, and Pa knocked his pipe loudly on the table.

They calmed down abruptly, tears streaming down their cheeks, embarrassment reddening their ears. "Oh, excuse us, the children. We're sorry. It's just this digging gets to you, is all. Think it's starting to turn us a little thoughtless, Jim. We're hardly used to being around women and children these days."

Brett punched the side of Jim's leg in a signal to leave. "We'd best be sorting our gear before dark. And thank you for the fine dinner, Mrs. Creath, and Doug, thank you for a piece of your river bank there to set up on. We'll be here a week or so if that's all right with you."

"No hurry," Pa said, standing to shake their hands. "Take your time. I'm not needing it for much."

Daniel stood up next to Pa. "Think I could come down and see your gear?" he asked.

Before the men could answer, Ma told Daniel he had things to see to. Rocks to put away off the kitchen table. Chores to do. It was the first time I realized how much Ma hated all this dinosaur business. She didn't want Daniel going down to the river. She didn't want him hearing this kind of talk. Maybe she sensed something then.

Maybe after you lose so many children, you begin to smell it in the wind.

G et down from there, this instant," a guard was shouting. Julia Creath and her granddaughter squinted up out of their late Nebraska afternoon to see Stevie grinning at them from the midst of the painted Indians who were rowing nowhere. He was high up, peeking out over the edge of the canoe.

"Stevie!" Ellie cried, jumping up from beside her grandmother. "How did you get up there?"

"Come down, Steven," his grandmother said gently.

The guard was huffing and pacing back and forth in front of them. "Is that your child?" he shouted. "How did this happen? Why aren't you watching him?" The Indians in their painted robes and fur vests didn't move. One stared straight ahead, not cracking the smallest smile beneath his animal head-dress.

"Steven, come down the way you went up, dear." His grand-mother stood there barefoot, and everyone watched as Stevie eased himself over the edge, his feet dangling in the air, and then he let go and landed at the feet of the guard, who im-mediately grabbed him by the scruff of the neck. "We'll have none of this—"

But the boy's grandmother removed the guard's hand from Stevie's neck as easily as she would peel a lizard off a warm rock by the river. "I'll take care of him," she told the guard, and before anything more could be said, she marched Stevie right out of the canoe room, with Ellie following—Ellie who was flushed with embarrassment, and who was once again carrying the old woman's black shoes.

Without a word the three of them marched out into the hall and up a flight of steps to the next floor. They didn't stop until they were far from the excited guard. Then the old woman smiled down at Stevie and straightened his shirt with gentle tugs. She was taking slow, deep breaths.

Stevie searched her face for anger and, finding none, sighed loudly. "Boy, Gram, I thought that guard was going to arrest us. Did you see the look on his face? I thought we were real goners."

"You *should've* been arrested," Ellie said. "You can't do that, just climb up on something in a museum like it belongs to you."

"What did you see, Stevie?" his grandmother asked. "What did you see up there with those Indians?"

His eyes narrowed and he tensed his body. "I saw the shore."

"The shore?" she asked. "What shore?"

"It was Australia. We were rowing to Australia, and I could see the kangaroos waiting for us."

"Is that right? Will they make it now without you?"

He looked thoughtful. "I think so. If I was arrested they wouldn't make it. Oh, no. But you rescued me, Gram. You saved my life. You did good!"

The old woman laughed.

But not Ellie. "Next time you might not be so lucky. I can imagine Daddy coming into the police station to pick us up."

"Oh, Elizabeth, Elizabeth," her grandmother said sadly. "How'd you get all these rules in your bones? You're only twelve. Where's your mischief?"

Ellie looked at the old woman blankly. Their eyes were almost level with each other.

"You know that afternoon I was just telling you about, when our mother wouldn't let Daniel go down the prospector's tent?"

"Yes."

"Well, we went anyway."

"You did?"

"Sure." She began walking along, an arm around each of them. "Daniel told our mother that he was going over to Jarvis's soddy, that the moon was full, and he'd be back late. And I followed him. But he didn't go to Jarvis's at all. He headed straight to the river and those prospectors' tent."

"Did you get in trouble?" Stevie asked.

"I sure did. No one knew where *I* went. They thought they

knew where Daniel was, over at Jarvis's, even though he wasn't. But after we'd been there awhile, listening to the stories, and watching the fire, I heard that old bell ringing on top of the soddy in the dark, real angry-like, and tore back there as fast as I could, but I caught it that night anyway."

"Didn't Daniel get in trouble?" Ellie asked.

"No. I told you my folks were sure he was over at Jarvis's."

"But you knew where he really was," Ellie said. "Didn't you tell them?"

"Why would I do that?" she asked.

The children looked up at her and wondered about the smile on her old face. She met their eyes. "You know what?"

"What?"

"It was worth it. It was well worth it, 'cause that was the night I saw who my brother Daniel clearly was. And I also heard all about that bad man, Hump Hinton. Things Jim and Brett never told Ma and Pa."

I watched Daniel that night from the door of our soddy. He headed over toward Jarvis's in the moonlight, and I kept watching till I figure he thought he was out of sight. Then sure enough I saw him cut back and head toward the river. I stepped inside the soddy where Ma and Pa were. I put on my sweater and carried out a wooden chair, making like I was going to sit a spell outside against the soddy wall, staring at the moon or watching owls or something. I made a lot of noise about setting the chair down in just the right spot, even tilted it back against the wall to catch the moonlight, and then I took off like a silent antelope after my brother.

The river was black in the night with swells of moonlight shining on the surface. It wasn't a deep river, especially then with the drought and all, but it was a wide river, wide and fast, and the sound it made was deeper than silence, quieter than the moon, like the sound of your own blood coursing through your ears.

The prospectors' tent sat up from the river a bit, all aglow from the lamp inside. I could hear them talking and moving around. I crept up close to the opening, careful not to get too close to the newly lit campfire. Inside, there were stacks of maps they were showing Daniel, and odd tools and brooms hung from the pole.

"How do you use this?" I heard Daniel ask.

And I watched as Brett leaned close and demonstrated a tool on the palm of Daniel's hand. "For more delicate work," he answered. And suddenly Jim stepped out into the night and saw me there.

"Well, well. What have we here? Another dinosaur hunter?"

"Don't have much use for dinosaurs," I answered. "Just wondering what my brother was doing."

Daniel peeked out from the tent. "Creath! Does Momma know where you are?" He'd always call me that around strangers, rather than say my name, Julie, he'd let on how he felt about me.

I narrowed my eyes at him. "She know where *you* are? *Creath*?"

We were all around the campfire then, and there were no real reasons to go on about why we were there. We just were, and the prospectors didn't question it, and Daniel wasn't going to make a fuss about it, so we all settled down around the fire. It glowed so bright that everything around us became black as if it didn't exist. All there was, was the fire, crackling and snapping, and somewhere low and quiet in the background, the river rushing past in the darkness.

Jim pulled out a flask from a knapsack on the ground and tilted it to his lips. He braced himself and seemed to stop breathing. Then he screwed the top back on and held it out to Brett, who shook his head, and Daniel, who smiled bashfully and shook his head too. He didn't hold it out to me, and I longed to just smell it. I'd smelled raisin wine once, and I had a feeling this wasn't raisin wine.

"So when'd you get this dinosaur fever, son?" Brett asked. "I was surprised to hear you even knew what a dinosaur was."

"Well, my pa told me about them a while back. About Howard Crow and these big reptiles thousands of years ago roaming the plains. And I've always liked rocks. Always felt they must tell a story somehow. Almost like they're books left by time for us to read, if we can just figure out the language."

I could see Brett looking at Daniel thoughtfully. "How old are you?"

"Almost sixteen."

Brett glanced at Jim and poked at the fire. "We've been thinking lately about taking someone else on, Daniel. Someone to help with the land search, and eventually to help when we have to hire and direct digging parties. When we finally find some bones."

I stared at Daniel's face in the light of the fire, his face two colors, black and orange, lit and in shadow, the known and the mystery. *Don't go, Daniel. Don't go with them.*

Daniel didn't say a word.

"It's a good life. You'd come along with us. See the country. We got plenty of money for food and gear. We'd get you a horse, and when we finally have a dig, Crow pays fifty dollars a month to each of the crew."

Don't go Daniel. Don't go.

"And there's nothing like lifting those bones out of the hard earth," Jim added. "Seeing each bone lead to the next, bigger and bigger, sometimes whole and unbroken since the beginning of time."

Daniel was silent.

Oh, please, don't go.

"What do you say, son? Are you interested?"

"Sure I'm interested."

The life sap drained out of me.

"But I'm going to stay right here and find my dinosaur."

He held his hands together as if he were praying, and they made me feel safe.

"I'm not just talking about finding one dinosaur, son," Brett said. "I'm talking about a life of searching and digging and adventure and good money and fame."

"I got a good life," my brother said. "I'm a farmer."

Choirs of angels clattered around my joyful head. I had

never heard my brother say those words before. *I'm a farmer*. It was like saying I'm an American, or I'm a Democrat. Imagine. My brother said, I'm a farmer, and at that instant, like being shown points on a map, I knew exactly where I was too. A farmer.

"All I want to find is one dinosaur," Daniel was saying. "My own. And I'll find it right here. On my own land. Like I do all my fossils. Plowing up the ground to plant, or digging a well."

"Or a grave," I reminded him, but he didn't seem to hear me.

"Farming's a hell of a life," Jim muttered, pulling again from his flask. "Nebraska ain't exactly the land of milk and honey."

"We got plenty of milk," I said. "And there's honey right now in these trees." I pointed up to the cottonwoods we were under, not really sure, but what did they know? And it was dark, to boot.

Daniel shifted his position. "So what do I do when I find my dinosaur? What's the first thing I do?"

"The first thing you do is, don't tell anybody." Jim lay down with his head resting on the knapsack. He held his flask in two hands on his chest.

"Nobody?"

"Well, just be really careful who you tell," Brett told him.

"Yeah," Jim agreed. "Like only your dead relatives." He snorted.

"You never know who's going to try to steal the claim from you, Daniel, and try to get the bones for themselves."

"And the money," Jim added.

"So what do I do?"

"Well, start by covering what you've discovered the best you can. With brush or mud. Keep it real natural, so that anybody sneaking around won't come upon it too easy. Then write a letter to Howard Crow. You have his address back east?"

"Pa does."

"Well, write him a letter and tell him, describe to him exactly what you've found. Tell him the description of the land. And if he thinks it's truly a dinosaur, he'll contact us to come look at it, or he might even come out himself."

"If he thinks it's the real thing, he'll be here himself," Jim said. "He sure as hell wouldn't want to miss the glorious moment of claiming it for himself."

"But it'll be mine," Daniel said.

"Yours originally. But wouldn't you want it to go to some museum or university and be reconstructed? Studied by great scientists, the top men? What are you going to do with a bunch of old bones? They can't mean anything to you sunk in the ground."

"You mean someday I'd get to see them all put together into a giant?"

"By experts who know exactly how to do it," Brett assured him.

"Experts," Jim snarled. "Experts who put heads at the ends of tails. Some experts."

"Would Crow pay for a dinosaur?" Daniel asked.

"Pay! Of course he pays," Jim said, pulling once more on his bottle. His voice grew soft and fuzzy. "Hundreds! Maybe even a thousand if it's good enough."

A thousand dollars, I thought.

"A thousand dollars," Daniel said out loud. "That could pay the farm's mortgage off."

"And buy more stock," I whispered.

"Of course, that's all up to Crow," Brett added.

But we didn't hear him. Not really. I was seeing Ma's face. Seeing her in a new dress. One with green and white stripes with the green still in. And I was seeing Pa strapping the plow to a strong horse.

"Unless Hump hears of it first," Jim said ominously.

"He the one with the camel you told us about?" Daniel asked.

"You see a man traveling with a camel and a Negro woman, hide your valuables. Hide your children," Jim hooted. "Hump Hinton's come to town."

"How can he have a camel?" I asked. "There are no camels around here."

Brett chuckled to himself and held a burning tip of a stick to his pipe to light it. "The great camel experiment," he said, between puffs on his pipe. The air gradually began to smell like apples and my mouth watered for autumn.

"The Army tried to use camels a while back down at Camp Verde," Brett told us. "Near Bandera Pass, Texas. Those dumb animals were strong and pretty useful as pack-train animals, but nasty critters, and dumb. Nobody wanted to take care of them, and you could say they fell out of favor with the soldiers. They were sold off, shot—"

"Stolen," Jim added, and then immediately snored.

Brett grinned.

"And Hump bought himself a camel?" I asked.

"Or stole it," Daniel said.

I hunched my shoulders up, hugging my arms around me, and tried to sense if anyone was sneaking up behind me, like a camel. Or a dinosaur. Or Hump Hinton.

"If you do find some interesting bones, Daniel"—Brett was looking intensely into my brother's face—"don't let Hump Hinton know. No matter what. No matter what he promises you. No matter what he says or how he threatens."

"What does he do with the bones?" Daniel asked in a hushed voice.

"He was hired by Mannity after we left. Mannity has no idea what he's got there in that man. He's totally ignorant, which is no excuse. But Hump should be behind bars."

"Why?" I asked, my skin already crawling.

"He shot a man, and nobody's caught up with him yet."

Something splashed in the river. A raccoon? A beaver? A murderer?

"Why'd he kill a man?" I whispered.

"For the woman he travels with . . . or a card game," Brett said. "I've heard it both ways."

And that's when the bell on top our soddy began its ringing—Ma'd discovered me gone. Like a bird flushed from the brush, I scrambled up and tore through the dark trees, up the trail and back to the soddy in the night. All the while I was running I thought I could feel a cold hand creeping along my shoulder. And all the while I was keeping a scream clenched in my throat, and the sound of camel hooves was catching up to me.

The dinosaur prospectors stayed on our land for nine days. For nine days they searched over our hills with their maps and their chisels, looking here and there, with Daniel following and learning. The two prospectors would point out where the hills turned color, the way the earth had been pushed up from underneath. They talked to whoever would listen, and that was quite a bit, since people came from miles around, gathering together at night in our soddy, for company, and for the sight of two new faces.

And then, on the ninth day, they were gone. They said there were no dinosaurs on our farm. It was a good spot, they told us, old dirt, but no dinosaurs. They asked Daniel once more to go with them, and when he said no again, that he was sure he'd find his own saurian, they took their leave.

Guess those dinosaur prospectors weren't so smart after all. But who knew the rain was coming? That awful rain that kept the soddy roof leaking for three days after it stopped. That fierce powerful rain that washed big chunks out of the creek bank and left those huge, smooth bones lying right out in the sunlight for Daniel, my brother, to find.

G randma," Ellie whispered. "Look."

While remembering old days and forgotten faces, they had wandered into another darkened room, their heads full of Nebraska hills and broken creek banks. But now Julia looked down at her granddaughter and followed her gaze into the center of a dark room where, incredibly, a herd of elephants rose into the air before them. Nearly a dozen giants stood frozen with their trunks raised, their heads arched up, inhaling, waiting to cry out, waiting for all eternity.

Slowly, Julia, Ellie, and Stevie walked deeper into the room, until they were very close to the elephants.

"Their eyes are marbles," Stevie whispered.

"And their tusks are yellow like old piano keys," said Ellie.

"Their ears are as thin as rose petals," their grandmother added, smiling to herself.

"Were there elephants in Nebraska, Gram?" Stevie asked.

"No, no elephants," she said, smiling. "Only that camel once. That was all. That was the strangest," she said, turning her back on the herd and sitting on the edge of the smooth wooden bench that circled them.

"I'm going to go look at the other scenes, Gram," Stevie told her, heading off to a glass case that housed a family of gorillas in a woody setting with a smoking volcano behind them.

"Don't go riding any hippos, now, Steven, you hear?"

"I won't, Gram," he answered seriously. "I won't do anything to get you in trouble. I promise."

"You ease my mind, son, you really do." Julia smiled after him, his skinny little legs, his corn-silk hair. Daniel would've enjoyed little Steven, she thought, settling herself back into the hard wooden bench that fit the ache in her back perfectly. Again she slipped her shoes off and sighed, gazing around at the dim and glowing displays in the darkened room.

Ellie knelt beside her, staring up at the elephants, imagining them suddenly coming to life, their bulky bodies moving forward, and their heavy feet continuing in their stride, as they would all head off together, going nowhere, as a clan.

"Why do you think they put skin on the elephants," her grandmother asked, "and not on the dinosaurs?"

Ellie looked at her. "Because they *have* the skin for the elephants," she said. "What I'm wondering is if there are bones in there, or if they just have the skin and stuff it."

Julia laughed out loud. "There *must* be bones in those elephants, Elizabeth. Else they'd look like a parade of baggy scarecrows. A bunch of stuffed toys. Like Eeyore," she added quietly. "Remember?"

Ellie remembered Eeyore from a quiet Nebraska afternoon, reading books out loud to her grandmother in her kitchen, while the old woman made wonderful concoctions of Jell-O and tiny little marshmallows and coconut. Nebraska. Ellie couldn't remember a creek bank though. Or a river.

"Tell me about Daniel finding the bones, Grandma. At the creek."

"Yes," she said, her face growing soft again with remembering. "I'll tell you."

It was after that rain, and the sun had finally come out once again. Ma and I were taking our things out of the soddy and lying them in the sun to dry—Pa's boots, the corn-husk mattresses, the wooden crates, even her sewing machine, the pots, everything. She wanted everything out of the soddy—to dry, to get the soggy smell out of there. Didn't matter to her that Daniel went off with his chisel and pick after helping with the bigger things, leaving me alone with her to make a hundred little trips. I didn't mind though. I laughed to see our things out in the sunlight, my clothes hung on the cluster of antlers by the door of the house, and Daniel's overalls hanging from the peak of the roof.

I was trying to arrange everything outside exactly as it had been inside, dragging the mattresses around, putting the chairs neatly under the table. I told my mother we should always live like that, under the sky, the stars.

"Near the wolves and the snakes," she answered. "Out in the snow and the rain."

It quieted me. Ma had her way of doing that, until Daniel came back. He was flushed and red from running, and I should have suspected something even then, but I was too full of myself.

"Look, Daniel," I told him. "Ma says we're going to live like this from now on. Outdoors. You get your own room if you want, over by the pump, and I get to put my bed right here under the sunflowers. What do you think?"

"Looks fine," he said, and I knew he wasn't listening to me. He was doing something strange with his eyes and his eyebrows, like he was trying to tell me something without words. I stared at him stupidly.

"The creek is full, Momma," he said, "Come see."

"Maybe later, Daniel," she said, not unexpectedly, her back to him, as she spread damp blankets on the prairie grass.

Daniel motioned with his head to me, secretly. "Go! Go!" it said.

"Well, I'm gonna show Julie, and I'll have her right back, Ma. Don't you worry."

He was backing away, a wild look in his eyes, his legs and

pants wet up to his knees. He beckoned me to follow. I left everything and ran after him, our mother's voice fading behind us. I couldn't keep up with him. I laughed. I laughed and laughed, the tall grasses whipping my bare legs, everything wet and yellow-green, everything so hopeful.

I slowed down as we neared the bank, but impatiently Daniel came back for me, swept me up like a calf under his arm and I bounced wildly on his hip until we slid down the bank together. We were mud from head to toe. Even half his face was covered with mud, and his teeth shone white with a smile like sunrise.

"Julie," he whispered. "Our dinosaur."

I held my breath. I think even the wind stopped blowing. I don't know what I expected. Maybe a slow dragon coming up out of a long sleep in the mud, but then I saw them. Like something mysterious and purposeful rising out of the mud, dark-gray bones, bigger than any bones I had ever seen in my life, jutted out of the broken creek bank. My two hands couldn't have spanned the circumference of one. Another looked like a dull shovel, heavy, rounded.

"Daniel!" I whispered. "Bones!"

"I knew there was one here," he shouted. "I knew it. I just knew it! And look." He fell to his knees and began burrowing with his bare hands in the mud. Almost instantly he hit another bone. Under the mud he gripped it, the muscles stood out on his arm, his foot slipped and sank deep, while he lifted a bone out of the sucking mud, a bone that was the length of a corn-husk mattress. He grunted, and it fell back into the mud with a splash. "It's all here! Everywhere I look! There's a whole entire dinosaur here."

"What'll we do now, Daniel? What'll we do?"

The two of us sat at the edge of the creek, on a patch of grass that was left.

"Well, Brett said to hide it. And not tell anybody. That's what we'll do."

"Not even Ma and Pa?"

"Not even. Not that they'd tell anybody, but I want to surprise them, Julie. Can you imagine their faces when we give them a thousand dollars for the farm?"

"A thousand dollars?" I whispered. "Do you really think there'd be that much, just for some old bones?"

"That's what Jim said. So we have to write to Howard Crow. You can do that, Julie. You're good at writing. Get that address from Ma's shelf, and we'll write a letter, and give it to Dolly to put in the next mail."

"Are you going to tell Dolly?" I asked.

"Heck, no! That old busybody?"

"Then what are you going to tell her you're writing about? You know she'll want to know. She looks over everybody's mail."

"Maybe we won't have to give it to her. Maybe we can be there when old Sy picks up the mail for the week. We can give it directly to him."

I frowned. That didn't sound so good. Sy never came on schedule. Some things on the prairie ran like a clock—the sunrise, the coming of the cranes, the first burst of sunflowers—but most things ran like crazy quilts, and Sy was one of them.

Daniel knew it. "Maybe I can tell Jarvis to keep an eye out for Sy, and if he sees him, come tell us. Sy has to pass his soddy to get to Dolly's."

"You'll tell Jarvis? Jim said don't tell anyone."

"I know, I know," he said. "We'll see. Let's write the letter first." Daniel looked at me, and a big grin broke across his face. "Wait till Ma sees you," he said. "You're mud from top to bottom."

I looked down at myself, mud on my skirt, mud on my arms, my feet. "You'd better come back with me, Daniel. So I don't get it."

"First help me cover these bones up," he said. "So nobody sees them."

Daniel and I pulled brush out of the muddy ground and stuck it around the bones. We patted mud where we could, covering everything, but the bones resisted. We pushed some rocks down into the creek. From a distance no one would know there was a dinosaur there. Close up . . . the bones called out to you.

April 23, 1885

Dear Mr. Howard Crow,

We are notifying you at once in the event of the discovery of a Dinosaur. We live by the Loup River in Nebraska. Also a Creek. It rained and now there are large bones sticking out of the Creek. Very large. We think for sure they are Dinosaurs.

*Jim and Brett are our Friends. You know our Father from
when you passed through once.*

*We would like to have the Reward for exclusive rights to
findings. Please come as soon as possible before someone sees
them. The Bones are rising out of the Mud.*

Julia Creath

"Want to sign your name too, Daniel?"

Daniel leaned over the table, and holding the pen awkwardly
in his hand he dipped it into the inkwell and pressed his
signature at the end of the letter. The letters were thick and
large: Dan Creath.

"There," I said, fanning the sheet of paper in the air to dry
it. "All we need now is an envelope and a stamp and we're
ready."

Daniel grinned and pulled both from inside his shirt. "Told
Ma I wanted to write to cousin Edward in Philadelphia."

"Ma would believe anything you told her," I said, copying
the address from the scrap of paper onto the envelope, and
then, licking the stamp, I set it in the corner. "There."

"And Jarvis said he'd come get me as soon as he saw Sy
coming through."

"You told Jarvis!"

"Only that I needed to see Sy, not about the dinosaur. I
told him I'd tell him someday, but not now."

"And that was good enough with him?"

Daniel nodded.

"That Jarvis Summerwaite's about as curious and interesting
as an old cow."

"But he's steady," Daniel told me.

I got up and hid the letter under my bed, between the mattress and the ropes. Daniel stuck the address back up on Ma's shelf with the other papers.

And we waited for the day that Jarvis would come and tell us that Sy was passing on the road, coming to start the two of us on an adventure that I would finish alone.

I t was pretty near dinnertime, the days growing longer and brighter, the sun nowhere near going down, when Jarvis came thundering in on his father's horse.

"Sy's coming!" he shouted. "It's Sy!"

Daniel and I jumped up from where we were sitting, and like a dust devil, I flew into the soddy where Ma and Pa were, whipped the letter out from under the mattress, and tore out the door. Daniel grabbed my hand and pulled me along.

"We'll be right back," Daniel shouted over his shoulder. "Gotta get a letter out!"

I looked back to see Ma come to the door and stare after us. "Julia?" she called.

"A letter to cousin Edward!" I shouted, but I didn't even know if she heard me. I just let myself be dragged along with Daniel. I ran, but with him pulling, my steps counted for more—I flew. Up and down the hills, around buffalo wallows, through stands of tall grass that burned my legs as I whipped through, all the while Jarvis and his horse fading off in the direction of his own farm. I gripped the letter in my hand.

Dolly's dugout came into view. Dolly. Now there's a woman who wouldn't have fit anywhere or any time in the world except on her own homestead, all alone, during those years. We could see her lumbering out toward her well. She was all over the color of Nebraska dirt, with heavy men's boots on her tremendous feet, and her hair matted and brown, like a bird's nest. She sure hadn't combed it—not to talk about washing it—in maybe years. Not maybe since she was little and her mother did it for her. If she'd had a mother.

Then we saw Sy coming over the hill in his wagon, ambling along like he was carrying the world on his shoulders. Dolly looked off at him, and then at us. Daniel waved to her, and she spat over her shoulder.

"What's in the mail that you two are all worked up about?" she asked as we came up close. Daniel secretly slipped the letter from my hand and left me standing there as he continued on to meet Sy. Dolly's face was gray and suspicious. She stood with her fists on her hips.

"We're waiting for a letter from my cousin Edward," I panted.

"In Philadelphia?" she asked. "The one with all the money?"

It made me twitch. "Edward's not got much money," I told her, my breath catching up with me. "There's nobody rich in my family," saying it like I was proud of it. Imagine.

"Anybody who doesn't live in this life-forsaken dust hole is richer than you and me," she said, squinting off at Sy.

I could see Sy leaning over the side of his wagon on the crest of the rise, to talk to Daniel, and Daniel was handing him the letter. Sy turned it around in his hand, checked the stamp, and stuck it in his jacket. Done! I thought. Howard Crow, you'd better be sitting.

"What's that brother of yours up to now?" Dolly asked, looking fierce.

"Momma had a letter for Philadelphia," I told her, hoping she wouldn't ask Sy if that were so. We waited while Sy and Daniel came down toward us.

"Help me bring the mail out, kid," she said, turning and disappearing down into her dugout. I followed her into the dirt burrow like a gopher. I wasn't used to dugouts, little holes dug into the sides of hills, and partly walled in the front with sod. I ducked as I went through the wooden braced doorway after her. Inside, it smelled like dirt and kerosene. There was a lamp on the table, and in the dim light she tossed a sack at my stomach. "Bring it outside," she ordered, "before that old scoundrel tries to get in here. I'll make coffee and bring it out."

But Sy was quicker than she was. No sooner had she said it, than he was in the door with Daniel right behind. The dugout was tiny for the four of us, and it was a great improvement when Sy lowered himself into the only chair. "So how are you, old girl?" he asked, wiping his hands along his thighs. "See you've done some redecorating around here. What's this in the corner here? A new pile of coyote dung?"

"If you don't like it, Sy, you can get your mail, drop your delivery, and move on out."

"Now how could I do that, honey, without some of your famous coffee? And besides, how would you know any of the gossip, if it weren't for me?"

Daniel and I exchanged glances. Dolly was pounding coffee beans in the corner of a flour sack with a hammer, all the while glaring at Sy. Then they started to talk business while Daniel and I tried to ease ourselves out the door.

"I just heard that over at Ravenna two hundred and fifty dollars was missing," Sy was saying. "Stamps and envelopes. Right out of Hans's safe."

"Serves him right," Dolly said. "That old Swede has no business handling government property—don't you two go leaving me here alone with this wildman," she said, looking up at us. But Daniel nodded and smiled and backed out the door, with a handful of my skirt.

We would've run, but something froze us in our tracks. It was Sy. He ignored us and said, "And then that camel over by Valley County. You hear about that?"

"Camel?" Daniel whispered.

We stepped back into the dugout, holding our breaths. Hump Hinton.

"Where was the camel?" Daniel asked.

"In Ord, creating a nuisance and a scene. Nasty thing, and

weird-looking. Can't believe God would make such a weird-looking animal."

"What do you know about what God would make?" Dolly snarled, pouring the grounds into her coffeepot.

"I know he made you, Dolly, don't I, and come to think of it, I guess if he could have made you, he could have made a camel."

I laughed in the yellow glow of Dolly's dugout, and looked away from her piercing eyes.

"Is it coming this way?" Daniel asked. "The camel?"

"S'pose so. The old guy who owns her says he's a prospector. And what do you guess? Gold? Diamonds?" Sy chuckled.

"Dinos—" I started to say, but Daniel piped right up loud and interrupted me.

"And he's coming this way?"

"Said so. And he's got a woman with him too, a Negress. Won her in a card game, I heard. Guess no one ever told her the North won. That the slaves are freed." He snorted. "Heard that the prospector won her from a trapper she lived with, and when that old trapper lost her to three aces, he accused this guy of cheating. They say the camel owner pulled out his shotgun and shot the trapper between the eyes. Just like that. *Boof!* Took off that very day with his camel and the woman. And no one's caught up with him since, although everyone seems to know all about him. It's like he's charmed, they say. The woman has some kind of magic."

"Imagine that, Daniel," I whispered, "right between the eyes." I rubbed my fingers between my own eyes.

Daniel shook his head, like a horse, to shake away flies or thoughts. We were quiet.

"Well, we'd better get back," Daniel said, pulling me out the door.

"Aren't you gonna see if you got a letter from your cousin?" Dolly asked. "Isn't that what you were all fired up about?"

"Actually—" Sy began, reaching into his pocket for the letter to Howard Crow.

"Yes, Sy," Daniel interrupted again. "Anything from Philadelphia?"

"How would I know that?" he asked, distracted now and pulling the leather satchel onto his lap. "Think I have time to read everybody's mail like Dolly here?"

Dolly snatched a handful of letters out of his hand and began shuffling through them. "For Edward Ely," she said, fanning the slim letter in the air. "Smell that pretty stuff? He's the one-eyed bachelor out by the cedars, and he writes to this lady in Boston telling her how beautiful it is out here, and how he's a rich landowner, and soon he'll have a spread fit for a king, and *she* gets to be the *queen!*"

Dolly and Sy laughed until Sy began to wheeze. "Wait till she gets here," he gasped. "Don't think Edward's had a bath going on three years. Think he'll shave to meet her at the station?"

"Hope she brings her lace curtains like the last one did," Dolly hooted.

She quieted as she peered at the next envelope. "Now what could this be?" She turned it every which way and held it up to the light. "Annie Taylor. Why, she left near eight months ago. After John died. . . ."

"Any from Philadelphia?" Daniel asked again. I could tell he was anxious to go. Maybe he'd want to pile some more brush on the bones now that Hump Hinton was coming.

She shuffled through the letters. "No. Nothing for the Creaths. No money from your rich cousin."

Daniel glared at her. He was as proud as I was. "Wasn't expecting no money," he muttered. And he turned and walked away with me a breath behind.

"Don't worry, Daniel," I said, like I'd talk to an old dog while patting him. "Don't you worry. We'll have our own money soon, from this old dragon on our own farm. Yes, we will. You'll see. In no time at all. That letter's on its way right now to that Howard Crow fellow. We'll be rich in no time."

"If Hump Hinton don't get here first," he muttered.

I matched my steps with his, but his stride was wider, and in no time he was far ahead of me. I watched his perfectly even heels kicking up Nebraska dirt. Then I watched his feet disappear into the buffalo grass.

Daniel. My brother. Soon he'd disappear from me, too.

When Hump Hinton first came through a couple of weeks later, Pa was away. I often wonder if Pa'd been there, if everything would have been different. Maybe he would have distrusted Hump and that woman right off, and wouldn't have let them stay on our land. But Ma was not so careful. Nebraska women were lonely and loved visitors. Loved any company. There was a woman we'd heard of, west of us, who was so lonely her husband found her one day sitting in the midst of their herd of sheep for company.

But Ma wasn't just lonely. She was frightened. That dark woman of Hump's had frightened her with what she seemed to know about Ma. And with her remedies. I can remember my mother's face during the days Hump and his woman camped nearby. Her cheeks seemed to strain across her bones unnatural-like and her eyes were always very black, like she'd been in a dark soddy for days.

I saw the camel for the first time from a distance. He was standing at our well, and I laughed out loud. The sight of him! The shape! The big hump on his back, and that funny, ugly face. I really forgot about Hump Hinton for a minute and called back to Daniel and Jarvis, who were straggling behind. "Look at this!" I shouted. "It's one of the three wise men!"

I looked back at Daniel, who stood motionless, a dead quail hanging from his hand. Our eyes met, and I knew. "Hump," I whispered.

Daniel caught up and handed the bird to me, all the while looking down at that strange creature by our well. "Give this to Ma," he ordered, "and whatever you do, don't say a word about the bones. You don't know anything about any bones. You hear?"

"I won't say anything, Daniel. You know that."

"That's even better, Julie. Just don't say anything at all. Come on, Jarvis."

"Come back," I shouted after them as they ran away. "Where are you going?"

"To cover up everything real good."

Jarvis and Daniel ran fast to the graveyard of dragons, and I knew that Jarvis must have known all along. I ran down to the soddy then, noticing something in the air, a peculiar smell, a stench, and as I drew close I knew it was the camel. He stood with his back legs wide, and broke wind loud enough to make me laugh, despite myself. I pressed my hand to my nose and ran through our door.

Hump Hinton and the woman were sitting at our table in the middle of the room. Ma was at the stove, chattering. She seemed uneasy and stopped talking when I came in and laid the quail on the stove before her. Its head hung over the edge.

Now if I were an animal I'd be an antelope. That's what I think. And if Daniel'd been an animal, he'd have been a wild appaloosa. The minute I saw Hump Hinton, I knew he would have been a snake. His hair was long and greased back, braided down his back, Indian-fashion. And he had an earring in one ear, a silver loop that moved when he spoke. He was wearing too many clothes, a leather jacket with fringe, and underneath about five shirts, with a large knife strapped to his hip. And I noticed his leg stuck out awkwardlike before him, as though he had a bad knee.

The woman with him was very dark, as dark and as shiny as a horse. The whites of her eyes glowed in the dim light of the soddy, and her teeth flashed like bleached bones. She watched me closely and said nothing. Hump Hinton felt the need to talk and be my friend.

"Well, here's a pretty little one," he said. "You sure do grow 'em pretty out here in this county. You folks have a responsibility, you know, for raising some more pretty women for these hard-working farmers. Yes, ma'am. It's your American duty."

The woman lowered her eyes.

"This is my daughter, Julia, and this is Mr. Humphrey Hinton," Ma said, "and his wife, Mrs. Hinton. Mr. Hinton's a dinosaur prospector, Julia. You know, like Jim and Brett. I was just telling them how Jim and Brett were here not long ago, looking for bones. And how Daniel has dinosaur fever. Crazy boy talks of nothing else."

"That's not true, Ma," I said, knowing she was saying too much. "Daniel hasn't talked about dinosaurs in a long time."

His eyes narrowed. "What did those friends of mine, Jim and Brett, think about the land here? Did they tell you?" Hump's eyes drilled into my head. I imagined he could see Daniel and Jarvis working in a panic to cover what showed.

I forced myself to look directly at him. "Said there were no dinosaurs here. None at all. Just some old fossils, a turtle, or two, but nothing big. Nothing worth anything."

"Such nonsense," Ma said. "Why would there be dinosaurs here of all places?"

"Of all places, this could be the most promising," he said. "Right, Amba?" He turned to the woman, who shrugged.

"Amba can smell dinosaurs," he told us. "And just as we were approaching your farm, she said to me, 'Mister,' she said, 'Mister, I can smell one. I can smell one long dead, and the biggest of them all.' "

I stared at her. How could she have known? I smelled nothing.

"This woman's spooked," Hump went on. "Can read minds, smell dinosaurs, even find water. Cure things. Say something, Amba. Give 'em some of your wizardry."

She shook her head shyly and twisted her fingers together in her lap.

"Go ahead. Tell this lady how many children she has."

Amba looked up hesitantly at my mother and their eyes met. I felt Ma shudder.

"Five," she said softly.

"Two," Ma said, too loud.

"Two alive," Amba said. "Three are gone."

Hump looked back from one to the other, a smile on his slimy face.

"They each died before the sun passed once," the woman added.

Hump knew by the look on my mother's face that this was the absolute truth. He slapped his thigh and guffawed. "What did I tell you? And she can give you something for that, am I right, Amba? You can fix her up a remedy so that her next babies don't die?"

"I could," she said.

Ma wrapped her arms around her chest and shuddered again. "I don't know," she said. "I don't know."

"Well, that's enough hocus-pocus for one day," Hump said, rising up stiffly to leave.

"You hurt your leg, Mister?" I asked, wondering if I could outrun him, if I had to.

"I didn't hurt my leg," he said, and then like a bad actor, too loud, too pronounced, he shouted in a phony voice, "It hurts *me*! All the time! Every day! Every hour! It's going to drive me to the lunatic asylum."

Before we knew it, he had whipped out the big knife from

his belt and plunged it into his thigh. Ma let out a piercing scream, her hands covering the sides of her head.

Hump was laughing. He posed for an instant with the knife protruding from his leg, and then he gripped it in two hands and wiggled it loose. No blood. No torn flesh. Amba had no reaction, she just hung her head. I'd the feeling this wasn't new to her.

"Wooden leg," he explained. "Lost it in the War Between the States. Always good for a laugh."

I wasn't even breathing. Amba kept her eyes lowered and mumbled thank-yous to Ma for her hospitality as she started to leave the soddy, but Ma didn't even answer her, just stood there with her eyes bulging, her hands still pressed to her ears.

"We'll set up down by the river, Mrs. Creath," Hump was telling her. "It's right nice of you to be so welcoming."

"I'll show you where," I said suddenly, wanting to draw him as far away as possible from the creek where I knew Daniel and Jarvis were working feverishly.

I lingered behind when they stepped outside. I looked back at Ma. Her lips were gray. "Momma!" I scolded. "Why did you tell them they could stay here?"

"I don't know," she whispered. "I don't know."

"They're saying he killed a man, Momma!"

"Who said that?" she said, as though she were suddenly angry at me.

"Sy told us. Said he shot a man between the eyes and took the man's wife—that Amba."

"Gracious," Ma said.

We stared at each other that afternoon, and it was almost like we were both hearing a distant rumbling in the ground, a roaring tornado that was destined to hit the soddy.

"Gracious," Ma whispered again.

And I went out to them.

aniel didn't believe me when I told him. "On our land? Ma said they could stay right on our land?"

"You told Jarvis?" I whispered hoarsely to Daniel. Jarvis was walking a little behind us.

"Yes, yes," Daniel said as if it didn't matter. "He just helped me cover the bones with brush."

I frowned back at Jarvis, who smiled at me. "You'd better not tell a living, breathing soul, Jarvis Summerwaite, or so help me you're going to find a skunk under your covers. So help me!"

"Oh, no," he cried, drawing his arms up over his face and head. "Anything but that."

"Come on, Julie," Daniel said, tugging at my arm and pulling me along toward the river. "What else did they say?"

"Well, Ma told him all about Jim and Brett—"

"Oh, no."

"But she told him Jim and Brett said there were no dinosaurs on our land."

"That's good. Then what?"

"Then Hump said that Amba, the woman, could smell dinosaurs, *smell them*, Daniel, and she had smelled one on our very farm. The biggest of them all, she said."

"I don't believe that," Daniel scoffed. "That dinosaur's been dead a million years. They don't have a smell. Rocks don't smell."

"But she knows things, Daniel. She knows things without knowing, like she can look into your mind and know just what you're thinking."

"Git off," he laughed, pushing me roughly by the shoulder, and I dropped back to walk silently beside Jarvis.

"Guess when she looks in your head she must see dust and wind and locust shells," Jarvis muttered under his breath.

"Well, no one has to look inside your head, Jarvis. All they gotta do is rattle it to know the truth about you."

Daniel led the way until we could see their campsite, and the three of us squatted behind some bushes together. The camel was standing off a far distance from Hump's tent, but we could see that his front legs were tied together and that he hobbled from bush to tree eating leaves, sticks, everything. While he ate, his tail swished at flies and he grunted and groaned.

"Would you look at that," Jarvis whispered.

Daniel breathed a low whistle. "Gives me a bad feeling," he said.

We looked back at the tent and watched as the dark-skinned woman stepped out, unpacked a canvas sack, and placed some tin bowls near the fire. She worked quietly and softly, and I wondered about her. Wondered how she felt about being won in a card game. Wondered if she knew she didn't have to be owned anymore. *I* wouldn't go anywhere I didn't want to go. Nobody could tell me what to do. I was just about to touch Daniel's arm and tell him that, when Hump Hinton himself came up behind us from the brush and the three of us nearly jumped right out of our skins and left them there.

Hump was standing with a rifle over his shoulder and a jackrabbit hanging from his belt. "Well, well, well," Hump said. "What have we here? A welcoming party? Or a lynching party?" He laughed at his joke, and the three of us stood up.

"Just bringing my brother around to meet you, Mr. Hinton. He said he could show you around our farm. And I told him about your old camel there."

"A weird thing, isn't he?" he asked, limping toward the strange animal. Daniel glanced at me with a distrustful look in his eyes. I nodded at him and motioned for him to go on.

"An Arabian camel," Hump was saying. He broke a switch off a tree branch as we approached. "Not a stupider, stubborner, nastier, dirtier mammal on the face of the earth. Ain't that right, Jack?" Hump hit him hard in the rump, and he squealed like a donkey, flapped his lips in a strange grunting commotion and didn't move.

Up close, the camel smelled worse than he had at the well. His eyes weren't like a horse's at all. He didn't look at us, but seemed aloof and arrogant, his eyes sliding away and his head held high. A rope was threaded through a pierced hole in his nose and Hump jerked it, but the animal still didn't move.

"Watch out now," Hump told us. "He's dead-eye accurate when it comes to spitting."

The three of us nearly fell over each other, backing up. Hump threw the switch down, slapped the camel hard on his rump with his bare hand, and motioned us to follow him.

He led the way to the tent where Amba was watching us. She held her hands clasped at her waist, and stood there waiting. I noticed that about her—that she always looked like she was waiting for something, and back then, I couldn't have understood what it was.

Hump flung the rabbit in the dirt near the fire and sat down to remove one of his boots. The one on his only good foot. He sat there rubbing his toes through his patched socks and moaning.

"Damned foot," he cursed. "Only got one and it gives me more trouble than most people have with two put together." He waved at us abruptly. "Pretty here brought her brothers," he said to the woman.

"Only one is her brother," she told him, her voice low and

knowing. "Not this one." She pointed to Jarvis while looking at me. She reached out then with both hands, two fingers pointing at both me and Daniel. I couldn't take my eyes off her. "This one," she said. "And the two of you have been together from the beginning of time. Locked together since all eternity."

I shuddered like I had seen Ma do, and looked at Daniel. I couldn't read his face. He was tall and blank.

"And you'll always be together, life after life, kindred spirits, mother-son, father-daughter, lovers, brothers, like two stars in the heavens that are always within each other's sight, whether clothed in sunshine or storms."

Always within each other's sight, she'd said. And I knew that myself, like I knew there were bones beneath the very meat of my own arms. Of course. I almost smiled at her, but she dropped her arm and kept one finger pointing just at me.

"Take care," she warned.

I saw only her.

"Don't put a harness on this man. You will only lose him. But build a fence around him that stretches to the farthest places of the universe. And he will always be yours."

I threw back my head and laughed. I knew that, I knew that, too!

"Why are you laughing?"

I looked at Daniel and realized he didn't understand. He didn't remember at all something I couldn't quite remember myself. He looked at me with an expression of total bewilderment, a look I had also always known.

"She's laughing because Amba knows all!" Hump exclaimed. "Knows all! Tells all! What a woman! If only I could bottle it somehow and sell it, Amba, you could make me a rich man. Forget about dinosaurs! I'd sell Amba Juice—guaranteed to cure what ails you, drive pain and discomfort from the human body, lead the way, and open up the truth and set you free!" His laugh was slimy, like a snake would laugh, if a snake could.

"Tell me, son," he said, a snake changing direction, "can you show me around your place here tomorrow? Like you did my good associates, Jim and Brett."

"Sure," Daniel said, and I could feel my brother's eagerness, his urgency to lead Hump all over and all around, but not to the bones.

Hump struggled to slip his boot back on. "Good. Good," he said. "I know there's one here, I just can feel it all around me. There's nothing like discovering a dinosaur. It's better than gold or silver, better than anything. A monster. A dragon. Ho-ho, I get itchy just thinking about it. Sit down, sit down," he ordered, pointing to the grass around the fire. "I'd invite you to stay for dinner, but I just got one old jack here." He pointed to the rabbit that Amba had begun to skin with a small knife.

"Ma's expecting us back," Daniel said.

"Wait, now wait," Hump said, suddenly patting his pockets looking for something. "Where's that poem, Amba? That dinosaur poem? Something I picked up in Ord, off the postmaster there. Wait'll you hear this."

"In your jacket pocket, Mister," Amba said. She never looked up, but split the rabbit open and cleaned him out swiftly with her fingers.

"Ah-ha!" Hump pulled out a soiled piece of paper and began unfolding it. "Sit! Sit!" he ordered us again. This time Jarvis, Daniel, and I squatted and sat together nervously. "Now listen." He began.

"A grinning skull first comes in sight"—he glanced up at us, his own grin ragged with brown teeth and black spaces.

> *"Armed with strong teeth, all shining bright.*
> *The spinal column follows fast,*
> *On either side great paddles cast,*
> *While a long tail of swimming form,*
> *Like a screw propeller it is borne.*
> *The mended bones show us the place,*
> *Where he was injured in the chase. . . .*

"Isn't that grand—" Suddenly Hump Hinton howled and screamed out in pain. "Bejeez! My foot! My foot!" he cried. Amba jumped up from the rabbit she'd been skewering and was at his side. The three of us stood up in terror. What was wrong? What was happening?

Swiftly, Amba opened his pants and reached inside along his wooden leg. There were snappings and straps and the wooden leg slipped out of the bottom of his pants. He wailed and howled, twisting his empty pants leg in agony. "It's the toes, the toes!" he wailed as if begging her.

"Be still," she told him. And the three of us stood there

with our mouths open as she proceeded to massage and rub a foot that wasn't there. She shaped her hands around air, and kneaded the invisible muscles and tendons as if she believed in them.

"Aaaah," said Hump, "Aaah . . ."

"Holy—" said Jarvis.

"Let's get out of here," said Daniel, and he and Jarvis were gone.

I lingered behind the briefest instant. Long enough to see Amba look up from Hump's phantom foot and give me the most cunningly shrewd smile I had ever seen in my life. That's when I ran. Took off, and didn't dare look back.

I'm hungry, Gram."

Julia Creath looked down at the small blond head in her lap and sighed. She stroked his corn-silk hair and rubbed his ear between her stiff fingers. For an instant she thought it was Daniel, but he was too small, no, her boy, Charlie, but no, not even Charlie. "Steven," she said to anchor herself in the moment.

Both children looked at her. Waiting. "Then what?" Elizabeth asked. "Did Daniel take Hump over the farm and keep him away from the dinosaur?"

Stevie sat up. "I'm hungry, Gram." His grandmother smoothed his wrinkled shirt.

"He sure did. He gave him the old banker's tour." The old woman laughed and her false teeth gave a funny clatter.

"Banker's tour?"

"Yes, you see, when a farmer used to go to a bank for a mortgage, he'd say, 'I have two hundred head of cattle,' when he really only had twenty-five. And then when the banker would come out to the farm to check on it, all dapper in his suit and shiny shoes, the farmer would put him in a wagon and give him a tour. He'd show him two hundred head of cattle, all right, but it would be the same twenty-five over and over. Once from the east. Once from the west, from the north, from the hill, from the gully, and the banker'd count them over and over, the same ones.

"That's kind of what Daniel did. He took him all over, to the river way north of the dinosaur, and then he showed him the hills where the earth had pushed through, and then he took him along the river south of the dinosaur and showed him where he found the turtle shell, all the while giving the impression that he was seeing the whole thing, only unlike the banker, Hump didn't see anything over and over, he saw everything, everything but the dinosaur grave at the creek."

The old woman opened her pocketbook and pulled out the map of the museum. "There must be a cafeteria here somewhere," she told Stevie.

Stevie peered at the map with her.

"Here it is," she said, smiling proudly. "Right down in the lower level. The cellar. I found it."

"You did good, Gram," he said, standing up and stretching. "I could eat an elephant."

"I'd be careful what I said around these guys," she said to him, jerking her thumb in the direction of the silent herd. She stood stiffly, slipped her feet back into her shoes, and held out her hand to Ellie. "Hungry, Elizabeth?"

"Look at this! Before we go! Look at this!" Stevie was pleading, tugging at his grandmother's arm and drawing her to one of the displays. He took them to a rhinoceros behind glass, posed motionless on the plains, rugged and hard. "Now what does that remind you of, Ellie?" he asked his sister. "That reminds me of something. I don't know what."

Ellie stared hard at the skin of the rhino. And remembered. "You must remember something of Nebraska after all, Stevie. His skin is just like the upholstery on the seat in Grandma's old pickup truck."

The three of them stood in the glowing darkness waiting for the rhinoceros to move or breathe. And it did look like the seat in her truck back home, Julia Summerwaite thought, and for the first time in a week, homesickness blew over her like a cold wind. She thought she smelled cattle. Grass. She would have to return home soon. As soon as she had told the children the whole story. After lunch. And after the dinosaur room.

The old woman and her two grandchildren left the elephant room and slowly made their way to the lower level, walking past red-eyed monkeys, arrowhead displays, and a giant whale suspended overhead from the ceiling, like a living blimp.

The cafeteria, unlike the frozen displays and silently posed animals, was alive with noise and light. There were crowds of people, lines for food, children running all about. Julia felt herself cringe inside. Too many people. Too much noise. A dull ache began to form in her head.

"Let's find a table first," she said, "and then we'll worry about the food." She searched around, feeling hopelessness rise in her like fever, until she spotted Steven jumping up and down by a corner booth.

"Here! Here!" he was shouting, while a couple were collecting their trays and sliding out of the booth. She smiled sheepishly at them, wondering if Stevie had rushed them away.

"Well, Steven, you did good," she said, collapsing onto the clean wooden bench. Her legs ached, a tremor shot up her spine.

"Don't sit, Gram. We gotta get on line and get food."

"I have an idea," she said, opening her pocketbook. She took out a bill and handed it to Elizabeth. "Get a nice lunch for each of you, and something to drink, and surprise me with something wonderful. And coffee. I'll wait right here."

She watched as they took off toward the lines, and then she withdrew inside herself like a turtle, pulled in her senses and her awarenesses, and closed her eyes. What would that old dinosaur look like today, all reconstructed and put together? She wondered if they had gotten the head on the right end after all, or if someone had put it on the tail. How clearly she remembered the smooth bones in the creek bank. The feel of them, the tremendous weight of them.

And then another memory came back to her, of that autumn afternoon not too long ago, when she had at last gone up to her attic and found the squirrel. Her husband, Jarvis, had been dead maybe ten years, and it had been almost that long since she'd been up there. There had never been a need really. Just Jarvis's army things. An old rocking horse. Dust. Memories.

But she'd gone up to see what was left of him. On a whim, because the autumn breeze had smelled like him that morning. She'd gone looking for Jarvis but found a message from Daniel instead. For there in a corner in one of the eaves was a dead squirrel who must've passed on right around the time Jarvis did. There wasn't a thread of flesh left on him. He was a perfect skeleton on a pale bed of tender fur.

Julia had been amazed at what she saw. The tiny skull, the hands pulled in to its chest, the curved back and the long delicate tail. It had looked like a dinosaur in miniature, and the hair on her arms had stood up, so close had Daniel felt at that moment. After Daniel had died she'd built many fences in her mind to hold him close to her, to contain him so she'd never lose him—fences to the moon, to the Rocky Mountains, to Venus, to the northern lights, and now there was one last fence to build—to New York, to that museum where the dinosaur was.

That was the day she began to think of young Elizabeth and Steven. Carefully, ever so carefully, Julia had slid a piece of heavy paper under the squirrel, not disturbing any of its form. She had meant to give it to Mabel's grandchildren, or to the boy across the street, but changed her mind. She sat in the dust of the attic. She didn't want to part with it yet. Not until she'd seen the real dinosaur. The big one. Daniel's.

*   *   *

Steven ran ahead of Ellie and slid into the booth like a clumsy little raccoon. His grandmother watched his fingers drum on the table as his sister unloaded the tray before each of them and handed over the change in a wad.

"Hot dogs, Gram. You like hot dogs, don't you? And I got you coffee, just a little cream like you like. And look! Carrot cake."

Julia Summerwaite, first-place winner of the Howard County Country Fair award for carrot cake thirty years running, looked down at the orange sponge on her plate and felt superior. "If that's carrot cake, Elizabeth, I'm Amelia Earhart."

"Who's Amelia Earhart?" Stevie asked, sauerkraut spouting from his lips.

His grandmother stared at him. "A lady flyer."

"*You* flew, Gram."

"Eat your carrot cake, Steven, and don't be so smart."

"Tell us more about Hump, Grandma," Ellie pleaded, smoothing her paper napkin in her lap. "Did Daniel manage to keep him away from the bones?"

Julia Creath was quiet for a moment. She picked half the sauerkraut off her hot dog and took a bite. The children waited. She sipped her coffee.

Not quite. Oh, he kept Hump busy all right, and all the while we were hoping and waiting to hear from Howard Crow back east. Every time Sy had come through, good ole Jarvis would come riding up to our soddy or wherever we were to let us know, and then finally one day, the third day Hump was camping on our land, and Pa was back, Jarvis came riding up to the front door.

"Daniel! Daniel!" he cried out. "I just passed Sy on the road, and he told me to tell you he's got an important-looking letter for you from New York."

I glanced at Ma and Pa at the table when Daniel ran to the door. They looked puzzled. "Why, Daniel, who would write—"

"Is he at Dolly's yet?"

I was at the door now too.

"Just about. Get on." Jarvis held out his hand to Daniel, who sprang up on the horse behind him. They began to ride off.

"What about me!" I shouted. "What about me!"

The horse circled back and Jarvis's strong fingers reached out to me, wrapped around my wrist, and mine around his. I was weightless, tossed in the air, and soon settled in front of Jarvis, the three of us pounding over the dry ground toward Dolly's dugout. "Faster!" I told Jarvis. "Faster!"

"Yes, ma'am," he said, and I swear that horse went slower.

Sy's wagon was already coming in view of Dolly's and she was nowhere in sight.

"You get off here and keep Dolly busy a minute, Creath," Daniel ordered.

Someone pushed me off the horse and I landed in the dust. "You'd better come back for me, Creath," I muttered under my breath, and, brushing myself off, I headed to the door of

Dolly's dugout. She was standing in the doorway like the rock in the tomb just before Easter morning, peering out at Daniel and Jarvis. How would I ever keep her from the mail?

"Have you got a minute, Dolly?" I asked. "I need some help."

She frowned at me. "And what would you be needing from me, Missy Philadelphia? You two keep hounding Sy like crazy. I'm just dying to see how much money your rich cousin finally sends you."

"No, it's got nothing to do with that." I slipped by her, into her dugout, and she turned to look at me as if she didn't trust me in there with all her worldly goods.

"What are you up to?" She squinted down her nose at me, distrustful-like.

"Well, I'm getting older now," I stammered and searched around for the right words, "and Ma and Pa don't really think I'm big. They treat me like the baby. You know what I mean?"

"I suppose I do. You oughta be pulling your own weight by now."

"You can help me, Dolly."

"How can I help you?" She crossed her arms over her chest and glared at me.

"Show me how to roll a cigarette."

"Ha!" Dolly tossed back her head and said "Ha!" She slapped her thighs and the room filled with dust.

I waited.

"Your pa would skin me alive."

"I won't tell my pa. Please show me, Dolly. Please."

There was the longest, quietest moment, a moment of horse hooves in the distance, and wagon wheels creaking. I waited.

I held my breath. Finally she reached into her pocket and pulled out her pouch.

"Sit down, kid," she said.

Julia Creath Summerwaite sat in the middle of the bright and noisy cafeteria. Her two grandchildren were entranced, their plates empty, their eyes full of memories they were hearing for the first time. Quietly, gently, as if they were sitting by the slopes of the river, they watched as their grandmother pulled out a pouch from her pocketbook. She selected a nearly transparent piece of paper from a packet, shook some fine tobacco on it, and with the same expertise that she fashioned quilted stars and shredded carrots, her old fingers rolled a perfect cigarette. They watched her lick along the edge, tap it down, and light it.

Grandma Summerwaite always rolled a cigarette after eating, and they had grown used to it, but now, suddenly, they were watching for the first time.

"Was it the letter from Howard Crow?" Ellie asked not of her old grandmother, who was making smoke rise in the air above them, but of the young girl she once was, the girl waiting for a letter.

"It sure was," Julie answered. "It was from Howard Crow all right."

"What did it say?" Stevie asked, kneeling up on the seat.

Grandma's face creased into a million old lines as she smiled at him. "It said: *I'm coming. Don't touch anything.*"

Т‌he heavy elevator to the dinosaurs was slow and silent. It stopped at every floor, and when the doors would open, people who had been chatting became silent as well, as they stepped in. The old woman felt the silence, was stunned by the silence that was as heavy as any she had ever heard. She thought maybe everyone knew, everyone knew where she was going and what she was about to see. The children stood on either side of her, and as the elevator left the third floor and rose, she began to hear Steven breathing, or was it her own breathing? She felt weak and placed her hand heavily on his shoulder.

The fourth floor. The dinosaur floor. Stevie held the map up before him and led them to the right, to the "Late Dinosaurs," away from Daniel's. She was glad, letting the little boy lead her, knowing all roads would eventually lead to the one she had come to see.

It was a bright room, so bright Julia thought for the first time that the rain must be all over; the sun had come out. Glass cases were positioned all around the room, and Stevie ran from exhibit to exhibit.

"Dinosaur skin!" he called. "Look, real dinosaur skin!"

"And look," Elizabeth said, pointing to another case. "Look at the horns on this one. Tri-cer-a-tops," she pronounced slowly.

Three dinosaurs stood in the center of the room, the tyrannosaurus towering above them. Stevie stood below its head, staring up at the teeth that would have each taken two hands to hold.

"Here it is, Gram," Stevie called to her. "Here's your dinosaur."

"No, that's not my dinosaur," she told him. "Mine was a brontosaurus."

"But is it here, Gram?" Stevie asked.

"Did you finally bring it here?" Ellie asked.

"It's here all right. But I didn't bring it," she said. "It wasn't so simple."

"Did Hump stay on the farm?" Ellie asked.

"Yes," Julia said almost silently. "He stayed around. For a while. He'd been on the farm about a week, digging and scraping all along the river, north of the bones, south of the bones, making Daniel near crazy. My brother became like a ghost, stalking Hump and that woman up and down the river, willing them away from his dinosaur, sneaking off in the night to make sure the bones were covered. He lived in constant fear that the wind or the dark clouds threatening rain would uncover them. He was sure Howard Crow would never get to us in time."

Then one afternoon the sky was black. Ma and Pa were both gone. They'd gone into town for the day to see to some business, and I woke up from a restless nap, thinking it was night, the soddy was so dark. But the old clock over the chest said half past three. It was still afternoon.

Then the thunder clapped right above me, and lightning flashed like a fire that lit up the soddy. I went out the doorway and stood in front staring out across the barren prairie. "Daniel?" I wondered where my brother was. Probably up with those bones. Making sure they were covered.

A stormy summer wind tugged at my skirt and fussed at my hair till I crossed my arms over my bony chest and shivered. Nothing. He wasn't coming. I held out my skinny arm before me and looked down it as I had seen Pa look down his rifle; my thumb was the sight. I looked for Daniel along the horizon. Daniel wasn't coming.

Looking back is like watching myself from a great distance. Maybe from the windmill. For the windmill watched me disappear into the dark soddy, saw my face appear briefly in the deep, sunken window, and then it saw me step from the soddy with Ma's heavy shawl wrapped about my shoulders.

My footsteps worried up little clouds of dust behind me as I set out toward the river. A hawk flew overhead and I pretended it could see me and Daniel heading toward each other over the rise. "Daniel!" I shouted, expecting him to come into view any moment. Didn't he have the sense to come home? Couldn't he see how dark it was getting? The lightning? How a storm was heading in? I walked faster, the shawl slipping off my shoulders, the fringe dragging in the dust.

Daniel would smile, I would see his wide shock of a smile from so far, and he'd hold up a length of line with two fish shining like silver goblets against the flashing sky.

I was running. I think I knew the worst even then, before seeing. Don't ask me how. My feet carried me forward, my toes dug into the dry soil. And very softly, like a caress, it began to rain. And I was running faster. When I came to the crest of the hill, then, I knew for sure.

Lightning flashed behind me, and there—before me, across the grasses on the way to the graveyard of dragons—was a streak of black charred prairie grass, and smoke rose from the streak like steam from a metal iron. And lying across the streak, smoke rising from his shoulders in the rain, was my brother. My Daniel. My brother. I knew. I knew. Even now, in the telling, my very lungs cry out, and I can feel the dead weight of him against me, in my arms, and the rain running off us both.

I stayed the night out on the prairie, on the trail to the graveyard of dragons, beneath the universe that Amba had talked about, and recalling what she had said, I built a fence in my mind for the first time, from cloud to lightning bolt, and then as the sky lightened toward morning, from star to star, so he could never truly be lost to me. I held my brother close until Pa came back the next morning and ran to the circle of buzzards that was still far up in the rained-out sky.

He came running toward us. "My God!" he cried, seeing Daniel's whiteness against the shawl in the cruel morning light. "Oh no, oh no, oh no." My father wept openly, lifting Daniel in his arms as if he were a small boy, and not almost a man. He started to walk home, and then he turned to me, sitting there in the mud.

"Julia," he said. Just "Julia," and I got up and followed.

Momma laid Daniel out on her bed and washed him. She didn't ask me to help her. She wanted to do it alone, but she spoke to me and Pa as she worked, and I listened to her voice and the sound of her wringing the warm water from the wash-rag into the metal pan of soapy water. Pa sat at the table, staring at the wall.

"I almost don't mind when a baby dies," she was saying between sobs. "Not like this. With babies all I remember is the shape of their heads, their sweet scent, but with Daniel . . . with Daniel. Daniel.

"I never thought he'd die. Not before me. Not Daniel."

The soddy was so thick with sorrow, I had to slip outside and sit beside the door, near enough to know if I was needed, but far enough away so I couldn't hear what she was saying, just soft distant murmurings. I was numb.

I rested my head on my knees, with no end to my tears. Even when I wasn't crying the tears kept coming, running down my neck, even down my knees and legs as I sat there. Pa stepped out and I looked up at him. I barely knew his face it was so twisted with grief.

"Tell me what he was doing out there," he said, not blaming, not angry, but just yearning, wanting to relive the last moments if he could.

"Remember that letter from New York that Daniel said was a big secret?" I asked.

Pa nodded.

"It was from Howard Crow."

We looked at each other and I could see on his face that he knew. "Daniel found his dinosaur?"

I nodded.

Pa held his hand out to me. "Show me, Julia," he said.

Together we walked away from our soddy, leaving Ma to dry and dress Daniel. The rain had given way to wide flat clouds that scudded across the sky above us, like large hands smoothing the earth down. The air was warm. My father's hand was warm. Sunflowers lined the path. They were growing tall, but had not yet opened.

Pa knelt beside me at the edge of the creek. Water was rushing through now, and as I gave a fierce yank at one dry bush, a large bone was exposed and the water began to wash over it and expose the full length. Pa saw it and took it all in—the large bone, the other places where I pointed, where I knew the paddle-shaped bones were.

"Why didn't Daniel tell us?" he asked me.

"He wanted to surprise you and Ma. Wanted to pay off your mortgage, buy some stock. Buy Ma a green-and-white dress."

Pa bowed his head and squeezed his eyes shut with his fingers. I wanted to touch my father, but I didn't.

"You know what, Pa?"

He didn't answer.

"Jim and Brett asked Daniel to go with them and become a prospector, did you know that?"

He shook his head, looking up at me then, his eyes like wounds. "He never said anything."

"He told them no, Pa. Told them he was a farmer." I smiled.

Pa smiled. "A farmer, huh?" The wind blew my father's hair up and away from his brow. He looked so young to me and open.

"Pa?"

The creek rushed on. My father stayed kneeling.

"Howard Crow is coming. He's on his way right now."

"Howard Crow," he said. He stood up slowly and looked up and down the creek. "That's good."

"But Daniel was worried about Hump finding the bones before Crow got here."

"Hump?"

"The prospector who's staying down by the river with that woman."

"Something about that man I don't like," my father said.

"Same with Daniel. Jim and Brett told us to watch out for him. And Sy says he even murdered somebody."

Pa's jaw hardened. "Why is your mother afraid of that woman?"

"Because she sees things. She knows things. Maybe Ma wanted the potion she said she had so Ma wouldn't lose any more babies."

"Aach!" Pa flung a stone across the creek. It made a hollow clunk in the water.

"But Howard Crow is on his way, Pa. He'll be here soon."

"That's for certain?" he asked.

"That's the letter Daniel got. It said not to touch a thing. That he was coming."

"Then we'll wait for him." Pa began covering the bone with brush, his hands trembling and his feet slipping in the mud. "We'll cover this up again for Daniel, and we'll wait for Howard Crow to get here."

We had a proper burial for Daniel. Had a minister come from Central City, and some others came, distant neighbors, Jarvis's family, Dolly, even some new folks who couldn't speak much English. I didn't want them there, strangers come to touch Daniel's thin wooden box and say inside, *Bless, it wasn't me. Not my son, thank you, Lord.*

I helped Ma lay food on the serving board outside when we came back from the burial place. I felt like I was inside a thick glass pickle jar, hearing things but not listening, seeing things but not really looking. People touched me, squeezed my shoulder, pulled my head against their chests.

And then Jarvis came back, his hands still dirty from filling my brother's grave. He took my hand. Strong and demanding, he pulled me away from the table while I was slicing a loaf of bread. I couldn't get free of his grasp, didn't try, and just let the bread fall on the grass. I let myself be led . . .

Until I realized where he was taking me. I pulled free of him. "I'm not going up there again right now," I said. "I can't."

Jarvis kept right on walking.

"You hear me, Jarvis? I'm not going there."

He didn't even turn back.

I had to run after him. "Jarvis, why are you going there? We don't have to go there today." I started to cry. "Oh, I hate you, Jarvis," I cried, and slipped my hand back in his, and he held it tight. He knew I wanted to go there, too. If Daniel were anywhere today, I knew he'd be with his bones.

Pa had covered the bones well, and even the rumbling brook couldn't uncover them. We stood at the bank, breathing hard. I felt the hot sun beating on our heads, the muddy water rushing by. Jarvis took his bearing for an instant, then, "Over here," he said. "Daniel kept the smaller bones over here."

He squatted down beside a boulder and dug with his hands in the dirt. Gently, he laid out a half dozen bones, some locked in rough stone, and some unbroken, smooth, sharp, the smallest the size of a tin mug. "Pick one," he told me.

I knelt beside him and ran my hands over the pieces. "Which one, Daniel?" I whispered. "Which one?" My hand stopped over a piece that was like a large rose thorn. I held it in my hands, weighing it, and looked at Jarvis. He nodded and hurriedly covered up the others once again.

"Done," he said.

"What are we going to do with it?" I asked.

Jarvis stood and took the bone from me. "Before the grass grows over Daniel's grave, we'll put it right in the dirt with him. Wherever this old dinosaur finally ends up, no matter who gets it or what happens to it, there'll always be a little piece missing. Daniel gets to keep one."

"Keep what?"

We spun around to see Hump Hinton standing a short distance from us. "Keep what?" he repeated. "What are you two up to?" He squinted at us and began moving closer.

"Run, Jarvis," I whispered. "Get my father."

But Jarvis stood stone still. "We were just looking for some kind of stone to put on Daniel's grave, that's all. His parents don't have any money for a good tombstone. Thought we'd find something we could cart up there."

"Why don't you come back home with us and have something to eat, Mr. Hinton," I offered. "Ma put out a spread, and maybe you could meet some people there. Tell them about your search for dinosaurs."

But Hump looked suspicious. "I heard about the kid," he said slowly. "That was too bad. A real shame. Not everybody dies from lightning, you know." He was moving closer to us. "Knew a farmer once in Kansas who was hit by lightning bolts twenty-nine times, and picked himself up each and every time." I could see Jarvis move his arm behind him, I could sense him tucking the thorn-shaped bone into his pants.

Hump came right up even with us on the bank. I could smell camel. He scanned the creek silently, his fingers tapping against his rifle. "The kid never showed me this creek," he said to himself. Jarvis and I glanced at each other.

I had to get Hump away from the creek. Had to make him forget he'd ever seen it. And then I did the thing that moment that came the most natural to me—I dropped my head back and began to wail. Jarvis stood there with his mouth open. Hump Hinton jumped back from me. "What the—"

"Oh, Daniel," I cried. "Why my brother, Daniel? Why couldn't *he* walk away from lightning? Why'd it have to kill him?" I put everything into my wailing. It wasn't hard. I cried louder and louder. I rolled my head back and forth on my shoulders, flapped my arms against my sides, stamped my feet. "Daniel! Daniel!" I screamed.

"Julie!" Jarvis shook me by my shoulders, but I wouldn't look at him. All I could think about was that bone hidden in the waistband of his pants, and the whole dinosaur lying hidden at Hump's feet.

"She's got the hysterics," Hump said, and I reached out for his hand.

"I want to go home," I sobbed. "I want my ma."

"All right, all right," Hump said nervously, as he took my hand and began to lead me away from the creek and toward the soddy. "Your mother will help you," he said. "Just get a grip on yourself, girl, stay calm now."

Slowly we began to walk back home. Jarvis was on one side with the dinosaur bone tucked out of sight, and Hump Hinton was on the other. I didn't pull away when he put his arm around my shoulder and rubbed me. I kept sniffling and sobbing, feeling like a snake had just wrapped itself around me.

"Come on now, Pretty," he was saying, "come on now."

Jarvis and Hump Hinton led me back to the soddy, and to the people who were gathered around in the front yard. When Pa saw us coming together like that he came up to me, scanning my face, reading my eyes, and for the first time I realized I was all that was left for him. I was his last living child. His rough hand cupped tenderly around the side of my neck.

"You look like you've been looped, lassoed, and branded, Buttercup," he said.

"She's taking it mighty hard, Creath," Hump said, squeezing me closer to his camel-smelling shirt, rubbing me, rubbing me. "Found her down by the creek crying her little heart out."

Pa's eyes met mine. Pa, Pa.

"You can leave her be now," he told Hump.

I felt Hump freeze. He didn't loosen his grip on me. "Just being fatherly to a poor hysterical girl—"

"I want you to take your hands off my daughter." Pa's hand was suddenly seizing Hump's shoulder in a viselike grip. Hump's hand dropped from my arm in a flash.

"Take it easy, you dumb sodbuster."

"Get off my land, Hinton," Pa said quietly. He seemed to swell, and gently he reached out and pulled me behind him. Jarvis joined my father shoulder to shoulder. I could feel everyone in the front yard hush. All eyes were on us.

"Hold it, now," Hump said, backing off and stammering. "There's still more I have to check. There's a whole creek the kid never showed me—"

"It's my creek, and I want you off it."

"No, sir," Hump said, shaking his head, not listening. "There's still more. I'm not done."

Quietly Amba approached him and slid her hand around his arm. "Come, Mister," she pleaded softly.

He shook her off violently, his arm snapping out at her, and she spun into the dust. "I'm not leaving," he snarled.

"Julia, get my rifle." It was Pa. He was talking to me. "Julie!"

"Yes, Pa, yes!" I turned, trembling all over, and ran to the soddy. His rifle was over the door, clean, loaded. I pulled it down, its weight turning my knees to water, and brought it to him, not seeing anyone, but hearing my mother.

"Doug. Doug, don't."

Everyone else was silent and still.

Pa took the rifle from me in both hands, and held it across him. He took a few steps back from Hump. Amba scrambled from the dirt. "Mr. Creath, Mr. Creath," she whimpered, "this is not for you to do." She was wringing her hands together.

"Get off my land," Pa repeated.

"Hold on a minute, Creath," Hump pleaded. "No need for gunplay. We can talk this out." He reached into his pocket and pulled out some rolled up money. He began peeling bills. "There can be a lot of money for you, if you just—"

Pa cocked the gun. I peered at Hump from behind my father's thick arm. Hump's face turned from polite begging to a sneer. His words were thick and slow like syrup. "You wouldn't dare, you chip kicker."

Pa slowly backed up, and the rifle raised in slow motion. Hump dared him with his eyes. The rifle lifted, someone whimpered. And then there was a shot that burst over the prairie like a clap of thunder. There was a muffled scream and then silence fell again as Hump looked down at his leg. His pants were torn open and his wooden leg was crooked and splintered like a broken wagon wheel.

"You're mighty lucky, Camel Man," Pa said. "I wasn't sure which leg was hickory and which was Hinton."

Hump stared at his leg in disbelief. Like he was waiting for pain that didn't come. "I got that leg in Philadelphia," he wailed. "Now what am I going to do? You son of—"

"Off my land," Pa said. "Next time you might not be so easy to hammer back together."

This time Hump let his woman slip under his arm and together they walked off, Hump limping and Amba bent under his weight. People drew close to Pa, patting his arm, nodding their understanding.

"Couldn't understand how you didn't get rid of him sooner," Dolly said. "Him being a known murderer and all."

Pa glared at her. "And how was I to know that? You got something against spreading useful information, Dolly, or do you just gossip about who's got lace curtains and who's got pleurisy?"

Dolly spat in the dust and, for once, was silent.

"Take my gun back inside, Julia." Pa held the rifle to me

and I carried it under my arm, like a hunter, letting its warmth rub against my leg.

It wasn't till much later, when everyone was heading home in their wagons and by foot, that Jarvis found me and asked me to go with him once again. The air was still and warm, and lightning flashed lazy and harmless off to the south. It was growing dark, and Ma didn't even notice me climb into the wagon with Jarvis, and no one saw the dinosaur bone nestled in the folds of my skirt.

"I can't stay away long, Jarvis."

"I'll get you back," he promised.

He took the path to the burial place, and in the silence of cricket song and wagon wheels grinding through the sand, I listened to the prairie. I had once seen a huge shell that I held to my ear, and they told me that the sound I heard was the sound of the ocean.

"Hinton's long gone by now," Jarvis said, staring straight ahead.

I nodded. "Jarvis?"

"What?"

"How come God never made anything that you can hold to your ear and hear the sound of a prairie night? Like hearing the ocean in a shell?"

"He *did* make something."

"He did?" I tried to see that boy's face in the starlight.

"He made prairie girls."

In the darkness Jarvis reached out and, taking my chin in his hand, he drew my ear against his ear, and our ears fit together like halves of a nut. "There," he whispered. "I can hear crickets and owls—"

I slapped his hand away. "You'd better leave off, Jarvis, or my pa will shoot you clear to Kansas."

Jarvis laughed soft and gentle, and somehow I knew we were both thinking of Daniel at that instant. We missed him. I held the dinosaur bone up before us like a beacon, and when my arms grew tired I let it drop back into my lap. My arm rubbed along Jarvis as the wagon rolled along, and I wondered if he *had* truly heard the prairie in my ear that night.

ike clouds rising from a riverbed, the sound of churning wagon wheels and crickets gently faded from Julia's mind, until she found herself an old woman gazing down into the eyes of two small grandchildren.

"Can I listen?" Stevie asked. Without waiting for an answer, or maybe knowing already what the answer would be, he tugged at her arm till she bent over, then he brushed a few stray hairs away from her ear and pressed his own ear to it. His ear was cool as a happy dog's nose.

"I don't hear anything, Gram." He tried. "Maybe you're too old now."

"Maybe," she admitted. "Except your grandfather claimed

he could always hear the prairie night in my ear. Right up to the end."

"I don't remember Jarvis," Ellie told her grandmother. "Did I ever meet him?"

"No," she answered, putting her arm around the girl's shoulder and feeling herself lean into the child for support. "He died an old man when you were just a baby."

"Did he know about me?"

"Oh, yes, your dad sent lots of pictures."

"Did he know about *me*?" Stevie asked.

"No, Steven, he died before you were born."

"I think he would've liked me though," Stevie said thoughtfully.

"I'm sure," she told him. Suddenly she felt like a bird that had just flown into a window and dropped to the grass. In one instant it was so clear that Jarvis was gone. Daniel was gone. She was alone now, and all that was left of those days was standing somewhere nearby, reconstructed, as if someone had taken the days of her childhood, strung them together like beads, and made a necklace for her. "Let's sit a minute," she whispered. "I have to sit."

The children led her. They weren't afraid. They felt her tremble against their arms and walked her slowly and carefully out to the hallway where old bones pressed in mud hung framed on the walls. Ellie remembered seeing her father come into the house once after working on pulling a tree stump from the ground in the backyard. His breath had been short and he was covered with sweat. She had stood next to him and felt the heat radiate off his body. She had thought, *This is what it is to work very hard.* Now she sat next to Juila Creath Summerwaite, her grandmother. She felt the coolness from her grandmother's skin. She looked at the woman's pale watery eyes, and her loose chin that trembled so faintly. *This,* she thought, *is what it is to grow old, and maybe to die.* And Ellie wasn't afraid.

"So what happened with Hump Hinton, Grandma? Did he leave for good then?"

The old woman leaned back and closed her eyes.

Something woke me in the early morning the next day. Half expecting Daniel to prop me up and slip me into overalls, I waited, until the awful sickness filled me, like creek water soaking into the mud. I knew with such clarity, such finality in that morning stillness that Daniel would never take me fishing again. I didn't open my eyes. There was the light twittering of birdsong, the distant creak of the windmill, and the steady sound of Ma and Pa breathing.

The air around me was heavy with dread. It grew till it was more than Daniel gone, more than a terrible ache. I felt a panic in the core of my stomach, like something terrible was happening. As if someone were disturbing Daniel's grave, I thought. My blankets churned like a chinook over me as I tossed restlessly, trying not to think of such things. But behind my eyelids, wolves were digging at Daniel's grave, tossing dirt between their wiry legs, tugging at bones with their bared teeth. We hadn't buried him deep enough, I thought, and whimpered. The wolves were stealing his bones.

Suddenly I was wide awake. I sat bolt upright and pressed my eyes open to the soft darkness. Daniel's bones. They were stealing Daniel's bones. And then, just like I had known that afternoon, when I started out looking for Daniel, I knew something was very wrong. Something terrible.

I leaped out of bed, stabbed my legs into my overalls over my nightshirt and ran out of the soddy, out into the pale summer air, and flew. The prairie stood still, turning slowly to my steps, too slowly, my breath came in hard rasps. I ran through the grasses, up the rise, and looked down where I'd seen the camel. It was gone. Their tent was gone, just a square brown spot where it had been. But they were still here. Like Amba could smell dinosaurs, I could smell camels. I dared not think the worst, but kept running until I reached the creek, and there stood the ugly camel, chewing his noisy cud.

Slowly I approached the cottonwoods, hearing voices, seeing movement through the trees.

"This is it, Amba! Look! Look!"

Her voice was softer and I couldn't hear what she said. There were splashing sounds, grunts. I hit my knees and crept along the deep grass to the edge of the cover. I drew very close to the creek, to Hump Hinton's voice. And there he stood, knee deep in creek water, his one shattered leg bound together with willow branches and rope. The new sun glistened on the water 'round his legs, and all around him were huge bones and stone pulled up, piercing the mud and water, shining in their innocence.

"Oh, Daniel," I cried inside. "Oh, Daniel, oh no."

I watched as Hump bent down and ran his hands over a huge bone he had uncovered, and then he stood up.

"I did it, Amba!" he shouted, turning to look at her and raising his arms in the air. "I have found the greatest saurian of them all!"

I dropped my head onto my arm, tears filling my eyes, such a terrible sorrow churning through me—when I heard a loud, ringing shot and what must have been the dull thud of a bullet breaking through Hump Hinton's chest, and I watched the red heart that bloomed through his shirt before he fell. Stunned, I looked back at Amba, who stood there wide-legged with a smoking shotgun held out before her in both hands. And as I stared at her, her head fell back and her arms collapsed. The gun slipped from her long, brown fingers, jammed in the dust, and leaned up against her boot like a good cat.

"And in your finest hour, I have taken it away," she said. And then she shouted up into the sky. "Jason! Can you hear me? I waited for just the right moment, and in his finest hour, I shot him down." She began to cry. "Like he did you. Like he did you." She crumpled like a rotten scarecrow into the dust.

Ice, ice, all over I turned to ice, and backed away out of the brush, churning like a frightened animal, never looking back. Just running and running, never stopping, even when the dark woman's wails encircled me like a snake and reached down into my throat.

✳   ✳   ✳

"And that was the end of Hump Hinton?" Stevie's eyes were big and dark.

Julia sighed and nodded. "And that was the end of Hump Hinton."

"What happened to Amba, Grandma?" Ellie's face turned to her out of her own pain.

"No one knows. They found Hump's body, but Amba was gone. Disappeared. Never seen or heard from again."

The three of them grew silent, and Ellie slipped her hand into her grandmother's old one.

"What about the camel, Gram?" Stevie asked, standing right before her and looking seriously into her eyes.

"What about the camel, Steven?"

"Where'd it go?"

Julia stared into space. "Guess Amba took it and went off on it. It's sure strange that no one ever mentioned seeing a small Negro woman riding across the plains on a camel now, isn't it? Maybe she just went up into the Badlands and disappeared." She grew thoughtful. "I heard this legend once sometime later about the phantom of a camel that's been seen galloping across the Great American Desert with the skeleton of a man on its back. Often thought how do they know it's not a woman?"

Stevie's eyes were as big as soup bowls.

"Did Howard Crow finally come?" Ellie asked.

"He certainly did." Julia Creath stood up then, the strength returning to her legs. "Indeed he did. And he took the bones away." She paused for a moment. "Would you like to see what he did with Daniel's bones?"

Both children stood.

"I'm ready," said Stevie.

"So am I," she murmured. "So am I."

Slowly they made their way down the hall. No one was around, and the echoing voices seemed to come from far away. There was only the soft murmur of their own footsteps. At the doorway of the Early Dinosaur Hall, the old woman took a deep breath and, together with her two grandchildren, walked inside.

Immediately before them rose the mighty structure of ancient darkened bones—the dinosaur, resurrected and pieced together. It was hard for Ellie and Stevie to imagine it all in parts, buried, and dirty in the wash on that Nebraska farm all those years ago. But it was not hard for Julia Creath Summerwaite. It was exactly as she had known it would be. Exactly. Hadn't Daniel explained it to her, sketching it out in the sand? Hadn't she seen pictures in his magazines? Oh yes, yes.

"*Brontosaurus,*" Stevie read from the plaque at its feet. "*One hundred and forty million years old, sixty-seven feet long, thirty tons. Found near Dannebrog, Nebraska.* That's you, Gram!" he shouted. "That's you!"

"That's me, all right," she said, and he leaned on her.

"Wow," he whispered from some deep spot in his soul.

Yes, she thought. *Yes.*

"Look, Gram," Ellie whispered. "He has toes like giant rose thorns."

Indeed he had. Julia walked to the side and studied the dinosaur's feet and the giant thorns. She looked around the room, then whispered, "One of those toes is missing, you know."

"Buried with my great-uncle Daniel, right?"

"That's right, and nobody knows except Jarvis and me, and now you and Stevie, so don't tell a soul."

Ellie touched a silent *x* over her heart.

"No one knows about Amba either," she said quietly. "About that morning at the creek. I never told a soul. Except you. Today."

Ellie trembled with the weight of it.

"Are you sorry I told you?" she said softly to her grand-daughter.

"No," was the answer. "I would have done the exact same thing."

"You would have?" The old woman searched the girl's face.

She was silent a minute and then said, "Thank you, Elizabeth."

Their eyes held.

"Now let me look at this big fellow," the old woman said, turning her face up to its tall skeleton. "Look at this. Look at this." She slid her hands along the cold metal railing and tried to see him from all sides. The gigantic bones and bony plates were bound together with metal clasps and bars, and its ribs rose in the air like a giant cage. His neck bones were like pointed beaks of a large bird, interlocking and growing smaller and narrower till they ended at the monster's eyes and a skeleton head. The old woman moved slowly around to the other side. The tail stretched out long and far, with more interlocking bones, growing smaller and smaller, fading like a coal train to an ending.

"A wonder," she sighed. "What a wonder."

"Look at this, Gram," Stevie called.

At the front of the dinosaur was a small replica of a dig, hard dirt with a bone emerging, and next to it a pick and a brush, and a wooden plaster box. "Just like Howard Crow's tools," she told them.

"I'll bet those are some of the actual tools that were used on your farm."

"Maybe, Stevie."

The room began to sway for Julia. The dinosaur leaned down close to her. "I have to sit, children," she said softly, and started for the only bench off in the corner. Some people drifted into the room, their heads tilted back, their guidebooks in their hands.

"Tell us about Howard Crow, Gram," Ellie said. "Tell us how he came, and what he did. Did he think you had a good dinosaur? Was Daniel right?"

Oh, Daniel was right, all right. His old dinosaur turned out to be the greatest find in North America in those days. It made Crow a famous man.

It was toward the end of summer when he finally arrived. The sunflowers were limp and heavy by then, leaning and rattling in the hard sunlight. I don't know why I didn't hear him coming, but when I stepped out of the cool soddy early one afternoon into the heat, there he was, perched in a wagon seat before me, a straw hat on his head, and a pleasant grin beneath his stiff mustache. He lifted his hat to expose a head as bare and clean as an egg.

"Would you be one Julia Creath?" he asked.

"The only one I know of."

"I'm Howard Crow, paleontologist and dinosaur hunter. I hear you have a cache of bones to show me." He smiled down at me from the wagon.

I think I grinned for the first time in weeks. He was really here, finally here. "Well, if you're hunting dinosaurs, Mr. Crow," I told him, "I've got one trapped and roped down by the creek that you're gonna love."

He laughed and started to climb down from the wagon. It wasn't till then that I noticed the four men with him. He was the only one dressed in fancy clothes, white shoes, thin pants, and a fitted jacket, while the rest of them were in heavy boots and thin shirts opened to the heat. They jumped from the wagon, too.

"Lead the way, my dear," he said, sweeping his arm before him. "Let's not waste another minute."

Without a word, I led Howard Crow and the dinosaur men out over the fields to the creek bed where the dinosaur was waiting. I can still remember the feel of the sun beating down on my bare head, and the crunch of the dry grass beneath the soles of my feet in those last moments. The tiniest doubts swelled up in me, like bubbles rising in batter. Maybe it wasn't a dinosaur at all. Maybe all this was for nothing. Daniel gone for nothing. Maybe Daniel'd been all wrong.

"Right here," I told him as we came to the creek. I waded in, stood where Amba had stood that terrible morning, and as she had pointed her gun, I pointed my finger. "It's all cast through the creek here, up into the bed, under the water, and even up under that boulder there." I waded to the other side, thrust my hands into a dried bush and yanked it out. Mud fell away, splashed into the water, and a long black bone caught the light. Howard Crow gasped. Without removing his fancy shoes, he waded right in the water, stood beside me, and fell on his knees before the stone. He ran his fingers along its surface, and gravely examined it through gold-rimmed glasses that clung to the bridge of his nose. He removed his hat to wipe his brow, and as he looked back at his men, the sun made his bare head shine.

Then he looked up into my face. I saw something familiar shining in his eyes, and waited for him to say something. But the men began to join him, pulling on bushes, kicking aside dirt, splashing through the water.

"I don't believe this," he told them. "This is one for the books."

"Look at this, Doc," one of the men said. A long thin bone jutted from the water.

Crow waded over to him. "I've never seen anything like this in my life," he said. "This is magnificent." Suddenly he turned to the men, paused, and before my eyes he transformed from an enthusiastic, starry-eyed scientist to a road boss. "All right," he shouted. "Let's not disturb any of this before we can sand-bag the creek, chart it, and see what's here. O'Malley, see if you can bring the wagon up close. Farley, how about some food? The rest of you, let's set up. Looks like we've struck dinosaur gold."

They all got busy then, going off for the wagon, getting their gear, finding an area to set up their tents. I was suddenly alone in the creek for the last time with the bones. All alone, and I was sad. I guess in my deepest heart I didn't want them taking the dinosaur. But for the moment, that last moment, it was just the dinosaur and me in an odd baptism of mud and memory. There we were, together, yet separated by a thick wall of time. I stood there and remembered tumbling down the bank with Daniel and seeing these old bones for the first time. A sob squeezed my ribs, and I wrapped my arms around myself for comfort.

"You do Daniel proud now, you old dragon, you hear? You be the biggest and the best old dinosaur that anyone's ever seen."

I stood there without breathing, knowing I was saying the first of my good-byes, and then I climbed up the bank without looking back.

he chain of events was in motion. There was nothing I could have done to stop it then, and I knew it. The dinosaur was no longer mine or Daniel's. We would sell it to Crow and his museum and it would be gone forever. All of a sudden it became important that I like Crow. Really like him. And trust him.

That night after dinner, Pa put on a clean shirt and said he was going down to talk to the paleontologist about payment for the bones. I combed my hair back tight from my face and waited by the well.

"Can I come, Pa?" I asked quietly as he stepped from the house. Ma would've said no. She hated the bones. But Pa nodded and I fell into step beside him.

"What do you think they'll pay, Pa? A thousand dollars, like Jim said?"

"Is that what Jim said?"

"That's what he told me and Daniel."

Pa whistled. "Let's not count our eggs before they're in the basket."

There were four tents set up by the creek, and the wagon had been unloaded of trunks, canvas, and loads of wood that would later be used for crates. Shovels and picks leaned against trees everywhere, like spears.

Crow stood outside one tent with a tin of coffee in his hand, gazing at the sunset. We walked into his long shadow, and he turned.

"Mr. Creath," he said, "I was just thinking of coming up to see you. It's a pretty nice sunset you've arranged for us this evening," he joked.

Pa shrugged. "It comes and goes."

Only I laughed.

"I want to talk to you about helping me put together more of a crew here. This is bigger than I thought, and I hope to get it all out before winter sets in. But I'll need more men."

"Not much of a harvest to work on this year," Pa said. "Men around here have time on their hands."

"I can pay fifty dollars a month. Full days of digging, crating, carting, sandbagging, plastering, hoisting. Sundays off, and we don't work in the rain."

Pa grinned. "No danger of that."

"Can you help me?"

"I can work for you. And get a few others."

"How many can you get?"

"Five, six men. Couple of boys."

Crow squinted off into the orange sun. "We've got to finish before December."

"And what do you pay for the bones?" Pa asked.

"I said—fifty dollars a month."

Pa looked straight ahead. "Your advertisement said there was a reward, and your man Jim says you pay for the bones."

Crow frowned and scratched the beginnings of a beard. "I'm afraid I've been misrepresented, and that advertisement you refer to is ten years old. The museum finances these digs, but there are more discoveries all the time, and there's just enough money to buy equipment, hire crews, and ship all this stuff back east."

"But Jim said you'd pay a thousand dollars!" I couldn't believe Crow didn't know, but he flinched and met my eyes, honest and open.

He was thinking. "Is that what you were hoping for when you found the bones?" he asked.

"My brother found the bones," I told him, and for cruelty I added, "but now he's dead."

"I'm sorry." Crow pitched the last of his coffee into the dirt.

"Is that why your son was looking for bones, for money?" he asked Pa.

Pa stared into the orange sky. The sun was gone. "No. He just loved bones. Rocks. Fossils. Anything old and mysterious."

"Please accept a hundred dollars from the museum," Crow said in a firm voice. "It's the best I can do."

Pa nodded. I couldn't speak.

"And gather up some men for me. We can begin work the day after tomorrow."

It was as if a circus had come to our farm. There were fourteen dinosaur diggers, Jarvis among them, and then other people who came from all over with children and baskets of lunch to watch.

The men were very nervous about the bones breaking, and now after months of carelessly wading across the creek, I watched as all steps taken were gingerly and light, as if the men were all walking across glass.

"Stand back there," the men would shout as little children scampered down the bank and crunched over the bones. Patience was thin. The sun was a steady, heavy roasting, and the men had to tie kerosene-soaked handkerchiefs about their heads to keep the buffalo gnats away.

"How big do you think these dinosaurs were?" a woman would call over the sandbags at Crow, while holding a small child tightly by the wrist.

"How many bones did they have?"

"Did they make a noise?"

The same questions again and again, and Crow never failed to answer them. Despite myself, and the anger I felt at not getting the thousand dollars, I liked this man's patience.

Ma didn't try to stop me from going to the dig. She liked

the company of everyone coming to our farm and stopping in to see her. There was always a pot of coffee brewing. She talked of Daniel to anyone who would listen, painfully at first, her face swelling and red, and then solemnly, and then I saw her smile once, point to the creek, and say something about "Daniel's dragon."

She hadn't talked to me about Daniel though. Not since the burial. Not since she had washed him and dressed him and I had left her. And each morning as I left her once again to go to the creek, I felt there was something happening inside her, a softening, a healing over, and although we never spoke of it, her words hung unspoken in the air, and I knew.

The place at the creek was no longer recognizable. The creek itself had been bent and twisted by Crow in a way it had never run before, and I could see my bare feet on the flattened grass on its bed. In places the creek oozed in from below, making everything muddy and cool, but Crow had truly lifted our creek and laid it down somewhere else. And then he had marked off the area with string and sticks and showed everyone how the dinosaur extended farther than we had imagined, had been bigger than we would have guessed.

Tools were strewn everywhere, picks, chisels, awls, brooms. I grew to know their names and their functions, and Crow let me help him with the gentle digging and probing, as long as I stayed by his side. He showed me how to mix the plaster of Paris till it was like smooth batter to pour over the bones. And I watched as he lashed the dry-coated bones with leather thongs that would protect them for their train ride east. He showed me how to number the plastered bones with a fat paintbrush.

Sometimes we would hear the bones creak as they were being taken from the ground. They would creak and then crack, an awful sound. But Crow would be there, pouring shellac over the shattered fragments of broken bones until they were of a piece again, ready to be carefully lifted and put with the others.

I watched as the men hoisted the plaster-encased bones with lifts and chains and lowered them into straw-lined wooden boxes. Crow trusted me to paint their numbers on the outside of the boxes, and even to record the numbers in his leather book.

Day after day I watched him, helped him, and listened to the same questions that he always answered. I tried to think of a different question, a question maybe he had never heard. One day I had it. I was gathering up the brushes and awls to put away for the night and I asked him.

"Tell me something, Mr. Crow," I started. I couldn't look at him. I concentrated on the tools, lining them up, brushing the dry mud off them.

"Yes?"

"Do you think these dinosaurs came before or after Noah's ark?"

He smiled at that one and scratched his bald head with genuine interest. "Good question," he said. "Can't say I know the answer. But I can tell you that in 1812, in Texas, before anyone had really found a dinosaur, or knew what one was, someone found a huge footprint in stone. Now we know it was a dinosaur, but you know what they thought it was then?"

I shook my head.

"The footprint of Noah's raven. Imagine that," he said.

I recognized the shine in his eyes, the same shine I'd seen in Daniel's. And I knew I forgave him about the money.

"Then when we began to know more, and got to study the footprints, to realize how big these creatures were, they were called *thunder lizards*, because when they walked they must have shaken the ground with every step."

Despite the late afternoon heat, a chill ran through me.

"And they walked right here," he said. "Right where we are now." He looked around him with wonder.

I understood that to him dinosaurs' fossils were more than money, more than jobs and bones in cartons. They were questions, a link with the answers he would probably never know about time and beginnings. But there was no thunder that afternoon, only the sound of the creek straining on its new path and the racket of birds.

I knew it was all right for Daniel's dinosaur to go with Howard Crow that day. And there was one more thing I had to do.

It wasn't till months later, on the very last night, that I brought them to him. The final wagons were all packed, the sandbags were emptied, and although the sandbags were gone, the creek had frozen along its new path. Most of the men were gone. Just a few were left to drive the wagons to the train. The heavy cartons rested silently on the wagon beds, their numbers indistinct in the darkness, their contents lifted from the mud for good. Howard Crow's tent was glowing yellow with warm lamplight.

"Mr. Crow?"

He was sitting at a small table, and he looked up at me from his ledger. He was in a heavy coat and a wool hat, with a scarf wrapped around his neck and face. I knew he was writing up the day's events, being a good scientist, and recording every detail. "Julie! Come in." He sounded as if he were glad to see me, and closing his ledger with his gloved hands, he motioned me to sit on the edge of his narrow cot.

I held out the sack I had brought. "These were Daniel's," I told him.

He took it gently and poured Daniel's familiar fossils and rocks out on the table. "Very nice," he murmured, "very nice." He removed his gloves and I saw that his fine fingers were blistered and cut now, and most of his knuckles were scraped raw, but he touched the rocks as a woman would touch the fingers of a little baby.

I sat there in the stillness with the man who would take away my brother's dinosaur, and here I was giving him Daniel's fossils, too. The inside of the tent shimmered as tears filled my eyes and spilled out over my cheeks. I wiped them from my chin and tried not to breathe.

Crow's gentle eyes took me in, and then he looked down at the rocks. And very slowly, like a storyteller, he began to tell me what they were. Which were fossils and which were old bones, which were the oldest, and which were plates from turtle shells. I didn't even listen. I just let his words run over me like water in the creek, smoothing everything in its path, calming, healing, while I sniffled and snorted and kept the tears from my cheeks with both palms. When he was done, he carefully returned the rocks to the sack and looked at me.

"You can keep them," I said. "My brother would want you to have them."

He nodded. "I'll see that they get put with the proper collections at the museum."

I stood to leave.

Outside, the early winter sky was blazing with stars. He followed me out. Orion's belt, Daniel would have told me. The Pleiades. The Big Dipper.

I pointed them out to Crow in case he didn't know. But then he showed me Saturn. Mars. And also a cluster of four stars at the edge of the Milky Way that he said was called the Riding Camel. He didn't know why my laughter cracked the night, but he smiled and we said good night.

The next morning the horses were harnessed to the wagons, and a few pack horses were loaded up as well. One horse ran off with a load full of bones and had to be brought back. I had wondered what pieces of the dinosaur would be missing if they hadn't caught him. The wagons creaked under the terrible weight and the frozen ground made it hard to turn. They had twenty-five miles to go.

Howard Crow was in a heavy coat, its collar lined with thick fur from an animal I'd never seen. He shook hands with Pa and even Ma and smiled at me before he climbed up into the wagon. He took the reins and pulled his gloves on tight.

"Mr. Crow," I said, stepping up and touching the seat of the wagon.

He looked down at me.

"You never said. What does dinosaur mean?"

"Terrible lizard," he answered.

"Oh, that's not true," I said.

"No." He smiled. "No, it isn't."

The other wagons were heading off, and waving one last time, Howard Crow fell in line and drove away. Ma and Pa went back in the warm soddy, but I stood there in the cold, shivering, till I couldn't hear or see the wagons anymore. Till everything all around me was empty. And the dinosaur was gone.

Until now.

Julia Creath was suddenly filled with a strange joy as she lifted her eyes to the brontosaurus before her. A terrible joy. If only Daniel could be with her now, to sit beside her, even if it meant he'd be an old man, just to see his life's work complete. A sob flooded the inside of her face and she gripped a child on either side of her. They held their grandmother's hands and looked at each other past her face. She had a look that old women should not have on their faces, and it startled them. It was a look of youthful passion and boundless joy.

She squeezed their hands once and then stood. An old woman in heavy black shoes and a navy-blue hat with berries, and a dark-blue dress with white dots, she approached the dinosaur.

Ellie and Stevie sat frozen like leathery stuffed Indians, their hands still shaped to hers.

As she neared the metal railing around the brontosaurus, her pocketbook slipped from her hand and she didn't stop to pick it up. She went on like a heavy prehistoric creature moving through mud and time. At the railing, she lifted a leg over it at the lowest point and then her other. She began to climb the base.

"Hey!" yelled the guard. "You can't do that!"

But Ellie jumped up and ran to him. She clutched his sleeve and motioned him to be quiet. "It's hers," she whispered. "She dug that dinosaur up herself. In Nebraska," as if that would explain it all.

The guard stood there with Ellie, and they both watched as the old woman made her way slowly under the proud head of the dinosaur. She reached up and tried to touch its chin, but it was too high. And the ribs were too high, but at the back legs she ran both hands up the shanks. She knocked on the bone with her knuckles.

"I don't know," the puzzled guard said. He looked around. No one was in the room.

"Oh, please, please," Ellie begged, never taking her eyes off her grandmother.

And then the old woman laughed out loud. The sweet laugh of a young child. It echoed in the hushed room.

Stevie and Ellie looked at each other.

"Oh, Daniel," she cried out. "We did good, Daniel! We did real good."

And then Julie Creath felt it, the hot wind on her face.

"Look, Julie, look!"

Was it really Daniel she saw, pointing across the prairie at three skinny, swirling columns of dust? The whirlwinds were dancing, bending, and graceful, as they wandered slowly from side to side over the grasses.

Daniel gave out a loud whoop and ran toward them, and Julie followed. "Wait for me, Daniel, wait!"

She and Daniel were so little out there where the sky touched the earth, but she was the littlest, so when they reached the whirlers all laughing and hooting, she had to turn her back to the hot wind and press into it. Her thin cotton skirt clung to her bare legs. She covered her eyes with her hands, and the dust stung her fingers.

"Spin!" Daniel was calling.

Julie squinted sideways at him and saw her brother spinning inside the whirler, his arms out, his brown feet dancing, and like him she held out her arms, backed deeper into the wind and went with it, whirling, spinning, laughing. And then there were children everywhere. She caught glimpses of them through the dust—Daniel and Jarvis, and even young Charlie and his sisters, and Elizabeth and that little boy, Stevie. Spinning, whirling, laughing, until at last only she and Daniel were left, spent and happy, lying on the dry summer grasses.

And then, breathing heavily and feeling the sun bake her smooth cheeks once more, Julie watched as the whirlwinds disappeared like good souls up into the wide prairie sky.